WHAT HAPPENS IN
POMPEII

MATT BUTTS

MoM Media Enterprises

Saint Louis Park, Minnesota

WHAT HAPPENS IN POMPEII

Printed with Pride in the United States of America.

Latin translations by Lingvanex. Cover illustration by ArtSpace.
Designed using Adobe software.

Typeset in 13 point Adobe Jenson Pro. Titles and headings set in Trajan Pro 3.

Proofreading and editing by Erick Crail.

By the gods, I do attest that this book is a work of fiction. Names, places,
organizations, deities, and events contained herein are figments of the author's
imagination, or are used historically and/or fictitiously. Any resemblance to
persons or deities living or dead is probably intentional, but as Jupiter is my
witness, I'll still deny it under oath anyway.

Library of Congress Control Number: 2023912169

ISBNs
  Hardcover: 979-8-9887027-1-9
  Paperback: 979-8-9887027-0-2

Also available for Amazon Kindle™
  ASIN: B0C4RP1RL7

First Edition — Idus Martii MMXXIV

www.mattbutts.com

To David Coleman
Whatever planet you came from,
please take me back with you.

"You might hear the shrieks of women, the screams of children, and the shouts of men; some calling for their children, others for their parents, others for their husbands, and seeking to recognise each other by the voices that replied; one lamenting his own fate, another that of his family; some wishing to die, from the very fear of dying; some lifting their hands to the gods; but the greater part convinced that there were now no gods at all, and that the final endless night of which we have heard had come upon the world."

— PLINY THE YOUNGER
From a letter to Cornelius Tacitus
Epistulae VI.20

PROLOGVE

POMPEII, 24 OCTOBER 79 C.E.

Marcus Andronicus awoke to the orange and golden morning sun streaming in through his bedroom window. His chest still ached from lying on the straw-filled mattress, and he could still hear the faint echoes of laughter coming from his master's *triclinium*. He rose from the bed and padded across the cold flagstone floor towards the balcony. The sun was bright in the sky, its warmth dancing on Marcus' skin as he looked out over Pompeii. The city was abuzz with life—the white-washed buildings, cobbled streets, and fragrant blooms all seemed to beckon him closer.

Back inside, Marcus filled a basin with water and splashed it onto his face and body, waking himself up. He then dried himself off with a rough cloth towel before donning his woolen tunic and leather sandals. Taking a deep breath, he silently descended the marble stairs, passing by his master's *triclinium*, where Salvius' laughter still rang out. Finally, he made his way to the kitchen at the back of the villa.

The cook, Flavius, had already donned his apron and was chopping vegetables in time with the clanging of the pans. He hardly noticed Marcus come in but motioned him toward a nearby bucket nonetheless. Marcus hefted it onto his shoulder without a word, tucking it beneath his cloak to hide the precious contents. Urine was a valuable commodity, used not only for laundry but also as toothpaste and mouthwash.

He navigated the streets easily, the locals giving knowing nods of recognition as he shuffled by. Finally, he stopped at the *fullonica*, a small building nestled behind neat rows of houses. The owner, an ex-slave himself, embraced Marcus warmly and handed over a few coins for the urine.

Satisfied with his morning's work, Marcus made his way to the market where merchants were busily setting up stalls for the day. Most of them knew him from childhood and exchanged pleasantries as they spoke about mundane topics such as Salvius's health or the state of Vesuvius. Through all of Pompeii's bustle, Vesuvius kept watch like an old friend—its rich soil made anything planted on it blossom and provide fresh food at an affordable rate. Marcus had climbed its peak many times as a boy living in Herculaneum, admiring Pompeii's beauty and dreaming that he would someday live there. Little did he realize then that fate would bring him there not as a citizen but as a slave.

He could have been a gladiator, an aspiration his parents had pushed him into at an early age. But Marcus was a kind and gentle soul who couldn't bring himself to do harm to another, so his disappointed parents sold him into slavery.

Marcus stood out from the crowd. His broad shoulders and dark curls made him appear more like a Titan than an ordinary man, yet he was joyful as he spoke to the vendors, moving about from table to table selecting only the finest assortment of fruits and vegetables for the master's pantry, sneaking a pomegranate for himself. This he sat down on a marble stone to eat, breaking it open against the rock and picking out its sweet, juicy pips. It was then that he heard the low rumble in the distance, coming from the direction of the mountain, and felt the vibration of the ground. These tremors had been coming with increasing frequency and intensity, and many were comparing them to the might quake that shook the city seventeen years ago; some cracked city walls still remained as a testament to its magnitude. This tremor was powerful enough to knock people off their feet. The rumbling grew louder and louder, building up to a deafening crescendo.

Then suddenly, deafening silence.

The people of Pompeii looked around, wondering what it all meant. Was it a message from the gods? What did they want? *"Deorum sunt iratus!"* a voice cried out. *"Pompeii peritura!"* Suddenly the mountain awakened with a mighty roar, a thunder louder than any thunder ever heard before, a sound so mighty it moved like a wall through the streets, piercing even the eardrums of the old and hard of hearing. Vesuvius belched forth a dark, ominous cloud of suffocating smoke and fire that obliterated the sun, raining down fire and brimstone on Pompeii and Herculaneum as their people prayed to the gods for salvation that never came.

CHAPTER I

There's an old joke I'm sure you've heard: Those who can, do; those who can't, teach. It's true in my case. My fascination has always been with the Roman Empire, since I was a boy studying it in school. I'm what you'd call a *romanophile*, an expert on all things ancient Rome. I can probably list every emperor who ever ruled the empire, from Julius Caesar to Romulus Augustus, including when they ascended to the throne and how long they reigned. I'm fluent in Latin, so I could read the writings of Ovid and Seneca, Tacitus and Cassius Dio, and both Pliny the Elder and his Younger nephew, usually in the original texts. I've seen Gladiator about a hundred and fifty times, and I can recite Marc Antony's eulogy from Shakespeare's *Julius Caesar* completely from memory, and my birthday, it just so happens, is the Ides of March. But I can't live in the Roman Empire, so I teach about it.

I'm pretty good at teaching, too. At 28, the job hasn't claimed my soul yet. My students like me a lot because I'm the cool history teacher who makes the lessons fun. Sometimes I take the centurion costume out of my closet (why it's there is none of your business) and wear it in class on casual Fridays. The students love it, and it shows in their grades. No student ever failed my class.

The energy in the room was palpable on the last day of school before summer. Students eagerly waved their hands, desperate to be called on, while I posed questions about life in ancient Rome.

The conversations ebbed and flowed as they shared anecdotes, facts, and stories that they had learned throughout the year.

"All right, class," I began, clapping my hands together to get their attention. "Let's see what you've learned. Who can tell me something interesting about ancient Roman culture?" Hands shot up around the room, and I pointed to a girl in the front row.

"They had really advanced engineering and architecture," she said confidently. "They built things like aqueducts and the Colosseum!"

"Very good!" I praised her and gestured to another student. "What else?"

"Roman soldiers were highly trained and disciplined," a boy near the back chimed in. "Their military tactics were super effective, which is why they were able to conquer so much of the world."

"Absolutely," I agreed, nodding in encouragement. As the discussion continued, I could feel my own enthusiasm for the subject growing. My passion for Ancient Rome and its history was contagious, and it was thrilling to see my students so engaged.

"Mr. Andrews," a random student called out, catching my attention. "If you could, would you want to live in Ancient Rome?"

I raised an eyebrow, considering the question. It was certainly an interesting one, and I had often pondered the possibilities in idle moments. I may have even had dreams about being a gladiator once or twice, but they weren't the kind of dreams I could tell my students about. "Well," I began slowly, "I'd be lying if I said I'd never thought about it. There's a ton about ancient Rome that has me absolutely hooked. Their artwork, their buildings, their stories... they all draw my attention like nothing else. But think about the tough stuff people had to deal with back then. Slavery was everywhere, women were treated like dirt and the poor were way worse off than the rich. Plus, no tech or medicine like we have now—which we usually don't even think about."

The room was quiet as my students absorbed this information. I could see their minds working, weighing the pros and cons of living in such a different time and place.

"I'm a pretty Germanic-looking guy, too. I'd probably stick out like a sore thumb in ancient Rome, ya think? They'd think I was a Visigoth." The class erupted in laughter, and I smiled at the thought of trying to blend in among ancient Romans. I couldn't help but feel a sense of satisfaction. My students had learned something new and interesting, and so had I—that despite my deep love for Ancient Rome, perhaps it was best experienced from the pages of a book or the walls of a museum rather than first-hand. Now came the fun part: I like to call the pee lecture. "Life in ancient Rome wasn't as pleasant as it looks in the movies. Did you know that in Ancient Rome, they used urine to wash their clothes? That's right. It was their go-to detergent. It's the ammonia, you see." You could see the shock on my students' faces when I mentioned it—priceless!

"Seriously, Mr. A?" one student exclaimed, her nose wrinkled in revulsion.

"Yep," I replied with a grin. "Yeah, not sure how I'd feel if I had to take my laundry to a public urine pool! Gross—but it did the trick. The ammonia in the urine apparently whitened up clothes and acted like a stain-remover. So, I guess it was kinda worth it? A laundromat would even buy your urine, so if you were flat broke, you could always sell yours. Some believe this is where the phrase 'piss poor' comes from. I kid you not." The groans from my students grew louder, and I could tell that I had their full attention. It was time to up the ante. "Here's another fun fact for you: the Romans also used urine to *brush their teeth*. They believed that it whitened their teeth." reply

An ad-lib chorus of "*Eww!*" was like music to my ears. "Mr. Andrews, that's gross!" another student cried out, covering his mouth as if he might vomit.

"But wait, there's more," I said, thoroughly enjoying the reactions. "Urine wasn't just for cleaning clothes and shining teeth—it was also used as a swig of good ol' mouthwash." The classroom erupted into sounds of disbelief and disgust, with students exchanging glances of horror. I knew I had them hooked, and it was time to deliver the final blow. "Oh, and one last thing," I added with an evil grin, pausing for effect. "It wasn't always *human* urine. Sometimes, they'd use *animal* urine, like goat or sheep."

The collective groan from my students was almost deafening, and I had to stifle a laugh. I could see hands flying up to cover mouths and noses as if the mere thought of ancient Roman hygiene practices was enough to make them sick. "Mr. A, you're just makin' this up!" one student accused, but I could see the glint of amusement in his eyes.

"Believe it or not," I said, shaking my head, "this is all true. Life in ancient Rome wasn't always glamorous, and there were definitely some aspects that we wouldn't want to experience firsthand. Don't get me started on their diet."

Before anyone could respond, the bell rang, signaling the end of class and the start of summer vacation, and not a nanosecond too soon. With a flurry of movement, my students hurriedly gathered their belongings and bolted from the room, still clutching their mouths and exchanging disgusted glances.

God, I love doing that.

"Have a great summer!" I called after them, chuckling to myself. "And don't forget to brush your teeth!"

I gathered my things, chuckling to myself as I locked the classroom door behind me. The halls of Emerson High School were filled with the echoes of excited voices and locker doors slamming shut, the unmistakable sounds of summer vacation beginning. As I made my way through the milling students, a familiar figure appeared in front of me.

"Ah, Mr. Andrews," Principal Luegner greeted me, looking me over disdainfully in my centurion costume. Given that it was the last day of school, he didn't make a case about it today. "Any plans for the summer?"

"As a matter of fact, yes, I do. An old friend from college invited me on an excavation of Pompeii she's working on. I'm sure I'll be bringing back all kinds of new information."

"Sounds exciting." The principal glanced down at my centurion costume and smirked. "Though your wardrobe might be a little... anachronistic, you think?"

* * *

My students don't know about my other life. Yeah, being gay isn't as big a deal as it used to be, and I could probably be out at work if I wanted to, but I just don't trust some parents not to make an issue of it, especially in this political climate. There's too much risk of somebody getting the wrong idea. I just don't wear my sexual orientation on my sleeve. And judging from the way the principal treats out gay students at Emerson—and we have our share—I don't think I want to be out at work. There are other gay teachers here that are more open about it. Let them be role models.

As I pulled open the door of The Saloon at Ninth and Hennepin, where I'm a regular patron, a wave of warmth enveloped me, and I stepped into a world of laughter and conversation. The vibrant clinking of glasses mixed with disco music created an inviting atmosphere, and people of all backgrounds were gathered around tables chatting away. Looking around, I knew that this was a place of acceptance—an oasis where I could be my true self without fear of judgment or discrimination.

It was Saturday night, and I was a man with a mission. I was looking for Mr. Right but would settle for Mr. Right Now. As much as I welcomed the chance to relax and make new acquaintances, I longed for more—for a deeper connection with somebody willing to accept me beyond my surface-level characteristics. I wanted to find solace in sharing secrets, dreams, and insecurities, but as these desires rose within me, they clashed against the realities of my life. Taking a deep breath to steel myself for what was yet to come, I decided to make the best of it. Or at least, that's what I hoped for.

I had been there an hour and a half now, but it had all been for nothing. I had approached several guys, but none of them seemed interested or excited by my presence. Some were outright rude, some said they had boyfriends, and some didn't even give me a chance to introduce myself before turning away. Worst of all was the one who told me he wasn't into me because he was straight. I wanted to scream, cry, and run away all at the same time.

I couldn't figure it out. Had I really changed that much? Was I too boring, or maybe even too desperate? Whatever it was, I was ready to go home and forget the whole thing.

But then, as I turned around, there he was. Will. My ex-boyfriend. Of the eight billion humans on the planet Earth, he was the one I least wanted to see. He had broken my heart into a million pieces, then lit the pieces on fire, then stomped on them. And I still loved him. He looked good, as he always did. His dark hair, his blue eyes, and his handsome face, all framed by a leather jacket and white T-shirt, made him look amazing. He seemed to be enjoying himself, laughing and talking with his friends. But when he saw me, everything stopped. Our eyes locked, and a wave of emotions swept over me: anger, sadness, regret... longing. He said goodbye to his friends and started walking towards me.

I didn't know what to do or say; I just stood there and waited for him to reach me. When he did, he just said, "Hi." Nothing else.

"Hey," I answered, feeling my guard go up immediately.

We just stood there for an awkward few seconds before he broke the silence. "Joe," he said softly. "It's good to see you."

"Is it?" I asked, unsure of myself.

He nodded slowly. "Yeah, it is."

"Why?" I asked, looking away from him.

He shrugged helplessly. "I don't know. It just is." We caught each other's gaze again, and he smiled nervously. "How have you been?"

"I've been fine," I lied, not wanting to show any weakness.

"That's good," he said without believing me.

"How about you?" I asked, ready for his reply to be just as false as mine was.

"I've been good, too," he lied in return. I could always tell when someone was deceiving me, but I was tired of playing the game, tired of digging deeper, only to find more darkness that desired to remain hidden within us both.

We stared at one another once more, and both looked around the bar as people had fun, danced, and kissed while we felt out of place. Will pursed his lips together before speaking first again. "So... are you here with anyone?"

"No," I said quietly. "You?"

"No," he replied, our eyes meeting once more in understanding and mutual acceptance of what we had come to find ourselves in – a loneliness that was masked by lies of 'being okay' and 'good' but being anything less than perfect was something neither of us wanted to admit to anyone else or ourselves.

A pause followed before Will shifted on his feet suggestively and cleared his throat again, slightly louder this time. "Do you want to... maybe... go somewhere?"

I shook my head firmly as if ridding myself of the temptation to give in to the impulse that lingered between us like a thick fog, heavy and suffocating yet alluring all at once. "No," I said firmly despite my craving for adventure that painted a different answer on my tongue. "I'm sorry, Willie, I just can't do it anymore. You're just too high maintenance."

Will frowned. "Take care, Joe."

"You too, Willie," I said softly before letting go of his grasp. He walked away from me back to his merry circle of friends, leaving me standing alone in the middle with nothing but broken dreams and a pounding heart.

I went home alone.

* * *

I woke up Monday morning to the first day of summer vacation. It felt good to hang around the house in my bathrobe. I had a few weeks to unwind before my trip to Italy, and I was going to enjoy every lazy minute of it. The morning mail brought a brown envelope with an international postmark, and it felt oddly thick in my hands. I regarded the envelope curiously, imagining it contained some invitation to a grand adventure, like in a story. I tore off the tape and opened the flaps eagerly, my curiosity piqued. I was right.

Inside was a plane ticket to Rome and a hotel reservation. My heart raced with excitement, and I quickly scanned the accompanying note:

Hey Joe,

Everything is set for this summer. Enclosed is your plane ticket to Rome, and we've made a reservation for you at the Hotel Montalbano. I can't wait to see you again. It's been ages. We'll have a couple days to ourselves so I can show you around Rome. It's about time you saw it for yourself, don't you think?

The real job is in Naples, of course, where we're excavating new sections of Pompeii. Your knowledge of Latin is going to be invaluable. As for Dr. Smith... well, you'll get used to him.

            See you in August.
            Kerrie A.

Kerrie Allison was an old friend from college, back from my days at Arkadia University. Okay, so we dated briefly, before I figured out I like guys better. I hadn't seen her in years, though we kept in touch over social media and e-mail. She was in Italy now, working on the excavation of Pompeii, and she'd used her influence on her mentor to get me hired on as an advisor on the project because I'm fluent in Latin. It was the chance of a lifetime, and I couldn't wait to get started.

* * *

I have to admit that in my study of the history of the Roman empire, the stories of Pompeii and Herculaneum have always been one of my favorite chapters. It's morbid of me to dwell on such things, but it can't be denied that volcanic activity has shaped human history. One of the first stories in the Bible—the tale of Sodom and Gomorrah—is basically a scientifically accurate account of a volcanic eruption when viewed through the lens of science. Brimstone is just an archaic word for sulfur, so "raining fire and brimstone" is just hunks of burning sulfur falling from the sky: that happens after volcanic eruptions: it literally rains fire and brimstone, just like it did on parts of Washington state after

Mount St. Helens erupted in 1980.

As I continued to pour over my history books, my mind began to wander to other tales of volcanic activity. I thought of the lesser-known story of Martinique, a small Caribbean Island devastated by the eruption of Mount Pelee in 1902. The eruption was so powerful that it completely destroyed the town of Saint-Pierre, killing nearly every single one of its 30,000 residents. Only one man survived: a man imprisoned for murder awaiting execution. They ended up setting him free, figuring that if God had spared him then he must be innocent. He went on to tour with Barnum because people love stories like that.

Back in 1815, Mount Tambora erupted in Indonesia, pumping so much ash and dust into the atmosphere that it caused winter conditions to persist through 1816, the year without a summer. Its effects are still known today. Trees grown during the "little ice age" produced the unique wood that gave Stradivarius violins their wondrous tone, and one teenage girl channeled her depression into what would become the first science fiction novel: that's how *Frankenstein* came to be written.

But my thoughts kept coming back to Pompeii, the ancient Roman city that was buried in ash and pumice after the eruption of Mount Vesuvius in 79 C.E. There was something uniquely fascinating and tragic about the way that the city was preserved, like a snapshot frozen in time. As a gay man, I couldn't help but think about the various erotic artifacts that were unearthed in the ruins of Pompeii, evidence of a society that was far more sexually liberal than our own.

As I closed my history book, I realized that I was feeling a strange mixture of excitement and apprehension about my upcoming trip to Italy. I was eager to see the ruins of Pompeii with my own eyes, to walk the same cobblestone streets that the ancient Romans had walked. But at the same time, I couldn't shake the feeling that there was something eerie and unsettling about the city, something that I couldn't quite put my finger on.

I'd probably remember once we were in the air.

I pushed those thoughts to the back of my mind as I got ready for bed, eager to get a good night's sleep before my journey began. But even as I drifted off to sleep, my dreams were filled with the ominous rumbling of an active volcano, sending shivers down my spine.

* * *

My bags were packed, and my taxi was on the way as I handed my spare key to Mike, my upstairs neighbor. "Felix likes to hide, but if you just shake the food bag, he'll come running. I just cleaned his litter box, so it should only need to be done once while I'm away." That's right; I'm such a romanophile that my cat's name is Latin for cat.

Mike nodded and took the key from me. "Don't worry, Joe. I'll take good care of Felix," he said, patting my back reassuringly.

Just as I was turning to leave, Mrs. Bitschlapp stepped out of her apartment across the hall. She gave me a disdainful look before turning her attention to Mike. "You better not let that cat scratch up my door again," she hissed, pointing a bony finger at him.

Mike rolled his eyes. "Don't worry, Mrs. Bitschlapp. I'll make sure Felix stays in Joe's apartment."

I could feel Mrs. Bitschlapp's beady eyes on me as I walked past her, but I didn't bother acknowledging her. I was just happy to be going to Italy. "You and your kind make me sick," she spat, her wrinkled face contorted with disgust. "Fortunately, by the time you get back, I'll be gone."

"What," I smirked? "You planning on dyin'?"

"No, but I'm moving out of this neighborhood. Since you perverts took over, I can't stand it here anymore."

"The feeling is mutual." Figuring it was the last time I'd ever see her again, I called out "Good riddance, *Canismala!*" as I climbed into the taxi and spoke to the driver. "Airport, please."

Someday she'll figure out my nickname for her means *bitch* in Latin. Or something close to it.

CHAPTER II

The moment I settled into my seat on the plane, I could feel the weight of anticipation pressing down on me. It was finally time for my dream trip to Rome—a journey I'd been dreaming of ever since I first started learning about the great civilization in fifth grade. I saw every movie about ancient Rome, from *The Robe* and *Quo Vadis?* to *Ben-Hur* and *Gladiator*. Now here I was, about to embark on the adventure of a lifetime. Who was I kidding? This wasn't s pleasure trip, it was a working vacation... even if I already knew I was going to have the time of my life doing it.

Assuming I ever got there.

"Attention passengers," an announcement crackled over the speakers just as I was settling into my seat on the plane. *"We regret to inform you that our takeoff has been delayed due to heavy traffic at Chicago O'Hare airport. We apologize for any inconvenience this may cause."*

"Great," I muttered under my breath, already feeling the frustration building within me. Let me give you some free advice—*never* book a connecting flight through O'Hare. *Ever.* I glanced out the window, watching the ground crew scurry around like ants, preparing the plane for its eventual departure. We spent three hours on the tarmac at Minneapolis-St. Paul International Airport waiting for O'Hare to let us take off. By the time we were wheels up and in the air, there was no way I'd make my connecting flight to Rome unless this bird had warp drive.

Hours later, when we finally landed in Chicago, I knew I'd

missed my connecting flight to Rome. The airline staff, who seemed as harried as I felt, redirected me onto a flight to Barcelona instead. While I appreciated their efforts, the prospect of waiting another six hours in the airport lounge only added to my growing impatience.

"Estne tibi forte nomen Augustum?" I mumbled to myself, trying to pass the time by practicing some Latin phrases. It was a feeble attempt to keep my spirits up, but it did little to alleviate the exhaustion that was settling in.

Finally, after what seemed like an eternity, I boarded the flight to Rome on a regional European airline I had never heard of. Images of ancient ruins, gladiators, and lavish banquets danced through my mind as I drifted in and out of restless sleep.

When I staggered off the plane in Rome, I was twelve hours late, jet-lagged, and running on fumes. Despite my exhaustion, I couldn't help but feel a thrill of excitement as I made my way through the bustling airport and out into the warm Italian night.

"Buona sera," the hotel clerk greeted me with a friendly smile as I gratefully noted that he spoke English. "Welcome to Rome."

"Thanks," I replied wearily, handing over my passport and reservation details. "I'm expecting a friend to join me tomorrow morning—her name is Kerrie Allison. Could you please call my room when she arrives?"

"Of course, *signore*," the clerk replied, his eyes flickering between me and my passport photo, probably getting the wrong idea about the nature of our relationship. But at this point, I was too drained to care.

Once checked in, I stumbled into my hotel room and texted Kerrie: "I'm finally here." Then, without bothering to unpack, I collapsed onto the bed and fell into a deep, dreamless sleep.

* * *

The morning sun streamed through the curtains of my hotel room, giving form to the golden filaments streaming toward me. I groaned as my eyelids opened and dragged across my eyeballs.

The sound of a phone ringing startled me as it echoed through the room. Sighing, I rubbed the remnants of jet lag from my eyes.

"Hello?" I croaked, struggling to wake up fully.

"*Signore* Andrews, your friend Miss Allison is here in the lobby," the clerk informed me.

"Huh?" I woke up enough to realize that I was in Rome. "Thanks, I'll be right down." I replied. I quickly splashed some water on my face and ran a hand through my disheveled hair.

As I stepped into the hotel lobby, I spotted her immediately. It had been years since we last saw each other, but Kerrie Allison was unmistakable. She stood tall and poised, her lean figure framed by waves of chestnut hair that fell past her shoulders. Her green eyes sparkled with intelligence and curiosity, and she carried herself with an air of determination that I remembered well from our time together at Arkadia University, a little college in the Louisiana backwater where we both matriculated.

"Kerrie!" I called out, waving her over. She grinned broadly and rushed towards me, enveloping me in a warm hug.

"Joe! It's so good to see you!" Her voice was filled with excitement, and her enthusiasm was contagious. She also had a gift for stating the obvious. "You look like shit."

"Yeah, I had an awful flight. Nothing a few gallons of coffee won't cure." I led her to a counter where coffee service was provided. "This is like a dream. I've always wanted to see Rome for myself."

Kerrie sighed. "I can't believe you're finally here."

"Neither can I," I replied, chuckling. "It feels like I've been traveling for days."

"Let's grab some breakfast and catch up," she suggested, leading me towards a small café near the hotel.

As we sat down with steaming cups of café Americano, which is what they call a plain old cup of joe here, Kerrie filled me in on her life since we'd last seen each other. After completing her degree in archaeology at Arkadia, she spent several years working on various excavation sites around the world. Recently, she'd joined a team uncovering new finds at the ancient city of Pompeii.

As we sat down in the cozy hotel café, the vibrant aromas of freshly brewed coffee and buttery pastries filled my senses. Kerrie ordered us matching cappuccinos, her eyes sparkling with excitement. "All right, Mr. History Buff," she began playfully, "I've got a whole itinerary planned for us. Since you got here late, we've only got a day, so we'll cram in as much as possible. We're going to visit the Vatican Museum, the Colosseum, the Roman Forum and the Circus Maximus. If there's time we'll go see the Trevi fountain this evening." She sipped her cup again. "So I hope you brought some comfortable shoes with you. Tomorrow we'll head to the dig site."

"So," I said as I sipped my coffee. "You said you wanted to pick my brain. Must be a really complex question if you flew me halfway 'round the world to ask it."

"I'm working on a dig site, and we need somebody who can translate Latin. You're the first person I thought of. It's the opportunity of a lifetime," Kerrie sat up a little straighter. "Right now about two-thirds of the old city is still buried; we've unearthed an area that seems to a small business. The inscription above the door says *Homines Domus*." Kerrie shrugged.

"Sounds to me like a brothel," I smiled coyly as I sipped my coffee. "One that caters to a specific market: men who like men."

"Sounds like your kind of place," Kerry smirked. "That's just the kind of thing we need your help with. Not just translation but interpretation. The inscriptions we've found appear to be written in a mix of classical and vulgar Latin, and I thought your expertise might be just what we need to unlock their secrets. I need someone who can read the inscriptions and decipher the clues. And when I thought of who I could trust with this task, your name was the first that came to mind."

I felt a surge of pride at being able to contribute my expertise to something so important. "When do we start?"

"Day after tomorrow," Kerrie explained, her eyes sparkling excitedly. "We want to understand not just what the inscriptions say but what they reveal about the culture and society of Pompeii during its final days. You'll be helping us create a clearer picture of life in this fascinating city before it was buried beneath the ashes of Mount Vesuvius." Hearing Kerrie describe the project sent shivers down my spine. It was a lifetime opportunity, and I could hardly contain my excitement. My heart raced with anticipation as I thought about the chance to breathe life into the long-forgotten voices of the lost city.

"Shh," I smiled, putting a finger to her lips. "You had me at Pompeii."

* * *

It was August, and all of southern Europe was caught in the grip of a record-breaking heat wave, with temperatures peaking over 40 degrees Celsius, which is about 105 on the Fahrenheit scale I'm used to. The sun scorched the ancient cobblestones of Rome as we strolled through the bustling streets, absorbing the vibrant energy that surrounded me. A bead of sweat trickled down my temple, but I hardly noticed—my thoughts were a whirlwind of anticipation for the adventure that awaited me in Pompeii.

Rome wasn't built in a day, but Kerrie and I tried to see as much of it as we could in one day before she was expected back at the dig site. She had made all the arrangements, eschewing guided tours and leading me through the sights of Rome herself. "Ready for your crash course in Rome?" Kerrie asked, her eyes sparkling with excitement as we stepped out of my hotel.

"Absolutely," I replied, my heart swelling with anticipation. "Where do we start?"

"We'll start with the Vatican Museums." Kerrie led me through the halls of opulent art and sculpture, priceless artifacts that included the spoils of other faiths, like a bust of Janus and statues of the Egyptian god Anubis among the treasures stored there. "A lot of these works were sabotaged by the Council of Trent in 1563," she pointed out. "They ordered any visible genitals or even pubic hair to be covered up by fig leaves. Fortunately, they never got hold of Michelangelo's *David*."

"Thank god for that," I smirked.

Next we took in the Colosseum. As we approached the colossal structure, I was struck by the sheer magnitude of it. Standing there, dwarfed by its massive walls, I felt as if I had been transported back in time to the height of the Roman Empire. It was supposedly even more wondrous back in its day, when it was covered in fine marble. In my mind's eye, I could see throngs of spectators filling the amphitheater, their cheers and jeers resonating through the air as gladiators fought for glory and survival.

"Did you know that the Colosseum could hold up to 50,000 spectators?" Kerrie said, breaking my reverie. "It's amazing to think about how many lives were touched by this place."

"Or how many ended here," I quipped, my imagination running wild with the stories that must have played out within these ancient walls. Gladiatorial combats and lions feeding on early Christians. The good old days. Now there's a big cross erected at the Colosseum in memory of all the Christians martyred there.

"Did you know," she said, her eyes lighting up with excitement, "that the Colosseum was built with eighty entrances to allow for the quick dispersal of the crowd? The 'vomitorium' wasn't where people went to throw up. They called it that because all those people at once looked like the exits were vomiting!"

"Wow," I murmured, gazing up at the massive structure in awe. "I can't wait to share that fact with my students."

"Come on," Kerrie beckoned, her enthusiasm contagious. "Let's head over to the Circus Maximus. You're going to love it there."

As we walked, my heart raced with anticipation. The Circus Maximus—the largest and oldest chariot-racing stadium in Rome! We arrived at the vast, grassy expanse, and I couldn't help but feel the exhilaration of the ancient Romans who had gathered here to witness breakneck races and daring feats of skill.

"Picture it," Kerrie said. "Two-horse chariots racing around the track, urged on by thousands upon thousands of fans chanting their favorite team's name. The noise, the chaos, the adrenaline!"

"I don't need to picture it," I breathed, my eyes wide with wonder. "You know I've probably seen *Ben-Hur* a couple zillion times." I smiled awkwardly. "I had such a crush on Stephen Boyd."

"Not Charlton Heston?"

"Eww," I sneered.

"I guess it's a matter of taste." Kerrie giggled. "Our next stop is the Roman Forum," Kerrie announced, leading me down a path lined with centuries-old ruins. As we wandered through the remains of basilicas, temples, and public spaces, she regaled me with stories of legendary orators, senators, and emperors who once walked these same grounds.

"Imagine Julius Caesar himself standing right here," she whispered, her voice full of reverence. I closed my eyes for a moment, feeling the weight of history pressing down upon me.

"With Brutus sneaking up behind him?" I struck a comical, dramatic pose. "*Et tu, Brute?* Then fall, Caesar!" Sheepishly, I added, "I bet all the tourists do that."

"Only the ones who've read Shakespeare," Kerrie smirked.

Later that day, we found ourselves in the *Musee Vaticani*, surrounded by priceless art treasures from throughout the ages. While I marveled at sculptures of ancient gods and goddesses, my enthusiasm was tempered by a nagging thought. "Kerrie," I said hesitantly, "don't you think it's ironic that an institution like the Vatican, which claims to promote charity and compassion, hoards such vast amounts of wealth?" I looked around the gilded hall of statues, most of naked men with fig leaves added later. "They could use these resources to make a real difference in the world."

Kerrie frowned, considering my words. "I understand where you're coming from, Joe. But remember, preserving these artifacts is also important—they're a testament to our shared cultural heritage."

"True," I conceded, though the thought still gnawed at me. "At least they were before the church vandalized them."

As we left the museum and stepped back into the fading light of a Roman afternoon, I knew that my journey through this ancient city had only just begun. There was so much more to learn, to explore, and to question. And tomorrow, Pompeii awaited.

As we continued our tour of Rome, Kerrie regaled me with tales of the city's storied past. We wandered through the ruins of the Forum, where the political heart of the empire once beat, and strolled along the remains of the Circus Maximus, where chariot races once captivated audiences. Each new site brought a fresh wave of awe and fascination, and I found myself more enamored with the city than ever before. We walked streets that were built during the reign of Julius Caesar, remarkably free of potholes.

"Okay, last stop on our whirlwind tour," Kerrie announced as we rounded a corner. "The Pantheon."

"Wow," I breathed, taking in the imposing *façade* of the ancient temple. "It's incredible to think that this was built nearly two thousand years ago, and it's still standing."

"Rome is filled with testaments to the ingenuity and endurance of the Roman Empire," Kerrie mused, gazing up at the Pantheon with admiration. "I think that's part of what makes it so endlessly fascinating—there's always something new to discover."

As we stood there, soaking in the history and marveling at the architectural genius of the Pantheon, I couldn't help but feel a deep sense of gratitude for the opportunity to experience Rome firsthand. This city, with its timeless beauty and rich tapestry of stories, had already begun to work its magic on me. And as I looked forward to exploring Pompeii with Kerrie, I knew that my journey into the past was only just beginning.

"Thank you for today, Kerrie," I said sincerely, turning to face her. "This has been an incredible introduction to Rome."

"Of course, Joe," she replied, smiling warmly. "And just think—tomorrow, we dive even deeper into history when we head to Pompeii."

* * *

The sun dipped behind the ancient rooftops, casting a warm glow on the cobblestone streets as we made our way to a small trattoria tucked away in a quiet corner of Rome. Kerrie had insisted that this place served the best pasta in the city, and after a long day of exploring historical sites, I was more than ready to put her claim to the test.

We made our way back to the Vatican, where we dined at a restaurant I liked because its name was Sarcasticus. Inside, statues of Barack Obama and Vladimir Putin in Roman centurian garb greeted us, while Silvio Berlusconi peered out of a chariot just inside the entrance. We sat and reminisced over what I believe was the best lasagne in the universe."

"Remember the Colosseum?" I asked as we settled into our seats, my heart still pounding from the exhilaration of standing where gladiators once fought for their lives. "I could almost hear the roar of the crowd."

Kerrie grinned. "And the Circus Maximus! Can you believe chariot races were held there over two thousand years ago? Talk about adrenaline!"

"Speaking of the Circus Maximus, did you know that it was actually built first by Tarquinius Priscus, the fifth king of Rome, before the Republic era?" I added, eager to share my knowledge with her.

"Really? That's fascinating!" she replied, genuinely interested. "You know so much about ancient Rome, Joe. It's no wonder you're such a great history teacher."

Our food arrived, and we dug in, savoring every bite as we continued to discuss the day's adventures. Between mouthfuls of lasagne, we traded stories about the Forum and the countless political dramas that unfolded within its walls.

"I couldn't help but think about all the power plays, betrayals, and assassinations that took place there," I mused. "Rome was like a real-life *Game of Thrones*."

"Exactly!" Kerrie agreed. "But let's not forget the artistic side of Rome. The Vatican Museums were incredible, weren't they?"

"Definitely," I nodded, recalling the breathtaking masterpieces we'd seen earlier. "Though I still can't wrap my head around the Church hoarding so much wealth when there are people starving in the world."

"Joe, you have a point, but remember that preserving art and history is also important," she gently reminded me.

"I'm just glad David isn't there," I commented.

"David?" It took a moment for her to realize. "Oh, *that* David—the statue. No, David is in Florence. I'm afraid that's not on our itinerary."

"That's okay; I have a life-size replica at home."

"Life-size?" Kerrie asked. "You realize it's seventeen feet tall, right?"

"Well, scaled down to life-size, then. Had the church gotten their hands on it, the pope would have them chisel off his pee-pee and put a fig leaf over it."

"Anyway, didn't the Trevi Fountain take your breath away?"

"Absolutely," I admitted with a smile. "I've never seen anything quite like it. How did that tradition go again?"

"Throwing one coin in the fountain is a wish to come back to Rome someday. Two coins is a wish to find love." With a smirk, she added, "And 'three coins in the fountain' is wishing for a divorce."

Then I should have thrown in two, I thought to myself.

"Speaking of wishes," Kerrie said, her eyes sparkling with mischief, "are you ready for Pompeii tomorrow? You know, they found all sorts of naughty frescoes and sculptures there."

I laughed, my earlier tiredness forgotten in the excitement of what lay ahead. "I'm a big boy, Kerrie. I can handle a little ancient debauchery. Besides, as I always tell my students, history isn't just about facts and dates—it's about understanding the human experience."

Raising our glasses, we toasted to a day filled with unforgettable memories and the promise of more adventures to come. In that moment, surrounded by the echoes of a civilization long gone, I felt more alive than ever before.

As our laughter subsided and we continued savoring our pasta dishes, I couldn't help but think about the upcoming adventure in Pompeii. "You know, Kerrie," I said, twirling my fork through the spaghetti carbonara, "I'm really looking forward to tomorrow. But I have to admit, my Latin training would make me sound like quite a snob to an ancient Roman."

Kerrie raised her eyebrows in surprise. "Oh? How so?"

"Well, I was trained in classical Latin, not vulgar Latin, and by some pretty persnickety teachers. I used to have nightmares about parsing verbs! Vulgar was more commonly spoken by everyday Romans, while classical was reserved for the educated elite." I grinned, imagining the scenario. "Imagine me strolling into a Pompeian tavern and trying to order a drink in the most eloquent, highfalutin Latin!"

We both chuckled at the thought, and Kerrie shook her head. "Ah, Joe, always the overachiever. But I'm sure you'll manage just fine. After all, you can figure out vulgar Latin, right?"

"Probably," I assured her. "It's basically just Latin with bad grammar, and I'm a teacher, remember?" I sipped my coffee again. "I find it amusing how different the two forms are. It's like… well, it's like comparing pig Latin or mock Latin to the real thing."

"Mock Latin?" Kerrie asked, intrigued. "I've heard of pig Latin, but what's mock Latin?"

"Think of it as a sort of humorous, nonsensical version of Latin," I explained. "For example, there's a phrase that says 'Semper ubi sub ubi' —which translates literally to *always where under where,*' but it's meant to mean *always wear underwear.*'"

Kerrie burst into laughter, nearly spilling her wine. "That's hilarious! Oh, Joe, you never cease to amaze me."

"Kerrie," I said as we stood outside the restaurant, the Roman night air cool against my skin, "I'm so stoked about going to Pompeii tomorrow. Can't wait to get a close-up of those old ruins—it's gonna be awesome!"

"Ah, yes, Pompeii," Kerrie replied with a mischievous smile, taking me by the arm as she walked with me. "You know, Joe, Pompeii was quite the 'sin city' of its time. A lot of the artwork you're going to see there is, well, not exactly safe for you to show your students, if you catch my drift."

"So I've heard," I smirked, coining some mock Latin of my own. *"Quod fit in Pompeii manet in Pompeii,"* I said with a sly wink. "What happens in Pompeii stays in Pompeii."

CHAPTER III

The sun blazed overhead, casting its searing light upon the ruins of Pompeii, now incorporated within the city limits of Naples. The ground and stones shimmered as if they were burning with heat. I squinted against the glare, wiping sweat from my brow as I stepped cautiously through the ancient city, the remnants of its streets baking beneath my feet. Heat radiated from the buildings as though they were emanating their own source of sunlight. We stopped at a small shop across from the entrance to the ruins, where we filled our canteens with cold water.

"All we really know about the eruption comes from letters Pliny the Younger wrote to Tacitus about twenty years later," Kerrie explained as the Italian landscape scrolled by the window of our high-speed train, which made the trip from *Roma* to *Napoli* in a little over an hour. "For a long time, it was believed that the eruption took place on August 24th, but we've found evidence that casts doubt on that date." She could tell by my wide-eyed expression that I was hanging on her every word. "First of all, we found a graffito scrawled in charcoal dated 'sixteen days before the kalends of November.'"

I did some quick mental math. Romans didn't express the date the same way we do. The months were pretty much based on the phase of the moon: the new moon (*kalends*), the first quarter (*nones*), and the full moon (*ides*). Thirty days hath September and all that, carry the one, and sixteen days before the kalends of November works out to…"

"October 17th, right?"

"Right. The inscription was in charcoal, which is about as permanent as chalk, so it would have worn away pretty quickly—unless somebody buried it for two thousand years. So we know it was recent." She looked up as the train began to decelerate into our station. "My personal theory is that somebody mistranslated Pliny's letter. They saw 'eighth month' and assumed it meant August. No copies of Pliny's original letter to Tacitus exist."

"The eighth month was October on the Julian calendar," I nodded. "The Gregorian calendar didn't exist yet."

"They believe the most likely date for the eruption was, in fact, 24 October," Kerrie finished as we arrived at our stop. "We'll get you checked in at the hotel, then we'll check out the ruins."

* * *

Vestiges of the city walls stared across the highway at us, beckoning us to come to Pompeii. We started out at a shop across the highway from the entrance to the site, where we stocked up on salty snacks and filled out thermos canteens with cold water. As we ascended the steps to the top of a stone platform, the ruins of the once-great city stretched out before us. In the distance, Vesuvius loomed over it, a giant bite gouged out of it.

As we walked through the crumbling walls of once-grand villas and shops, their faded gilt decorations and frescoes whispered secrets of a world long gone. The aroma of life in another time clung to every surface like incense in the air—a sweet, musky scent that mingled with the smell of damp earth. Despite the passage of time and the devastation that had befallen this place, there was still something hauntingly beautiful about it all. Standing amidst the silent ruins brought me face-to-face with an entirely new side of human experience, one which compelled me to look past my own cultural prejudices and acknowledge how very similar we all were. These people, whom I had studied in books for so many years, now became real to me. As I walked through the streets and plazas, surrounded by death, I felt like I was being watched by unseen eyes—eyes that wanted me to remember them.

"Look at Vesuvius, Joe," The massive cap of the volcano was visible in the distance, like an all-seeing eye. A wispy cloud behind it gave the illusion of steam rising from the caldera. Its peak was sawtooth-like and there was a gaping hole carved into its side as if a bite had been taken out of it—a tell-tale sign of the eruption that had destroyed Pompeii two thousand years before our feet touched its ash-ridden streets. A ferocious wind blew through the valley, from one end to the other. When we looked below us, we could see buildings made of small brick walls with roofs made of wood or tiles—they were a brilliant gold color. As soon as we visited Pompeii, we realized this was another city of rich merchants; for many centuries now, they had been extracting copper from nearby mines in order to feed Roman taste for better bronze weapons.

"Hard to believe it caused all this destruction," I murmured, thinking back to the tales I'd shared with my students about the catastrophic eruption. My fingers brushed against the rough texture of Pompeii's stones, tracing the grooves left by countless hands before mine. The weight of the past pressed down on me, heavy and inescapable.

Kerrie and I exchanged a silent nod of understanding, both of us having a shared appreciation for history, even if our studies had taken us down different paths. As we ventured through the ruins, my mind was in turmoil; I tried to imagine how life must have been when the city was bustling with activity, feeling a deep sadness that all of it had vanished.

"Hey, check this out," Kerrie called, pulling me from my reverie. She was standing next to a small shrine, its stones worn smooth by time and countless touches. I could see the faint outline of an inscription, and my heart leaped with excitement as I realized it was written in Latin.

"Let's see..." I muttered, studying the ancient text. "It says, 'May the gods watch over our beloved city and protect us from disaster.'" The irony of the words sent a shiver up my spine. If only they'd known...

"Looks like their prayers weren't answered," Kerrie sighed, her voice tinged with sadness. "Poor souls."

"Perhaps not," I agreed quietly, feeling a sudden, inexplicable pang of grief for the people who had perished here so long ago. "But at least we can honor their memory by learning from their past."

As we continued exploring the ruins, I spotted two men approaching from a distance. The taller of the two had a swagger to his walk, with a wide-brimmed hat shading his face and a gold chain glinting around his neck. His assistant was of average height, with glasses perched on his nose and a satchel slung over his shoulder.

"Joe!" Kerrie said, waving me over. "I want you to meet my mentor, Dr. Cal—"

"California Smith," he crowed proudly, grabbing my hand and squeezing tightly enough to crack a metacarpal or two. "Nice to meet ya, kid," Dr. Smith drawled, extending a hand adorned with numerous rings. His grip was firm, almost bruising, and I could see the predatory gleam in his eyes as he assessed me. "Looks like you and Miles are gonna be thick as thieves, huh?"

"Actually, it's Niles," his assistant corrected, but Dr. Smith seemed not to hear him.

"Dr. Smith is an expert on Roman antiquities," Kerrie said, clearly admiring her mentor despite his rough demeanor. "He's written several books on the subject."

"Indeed," Dr. Smith replied, puffing out his chest. "And Pompeii is just the latest feather in my cap. There's so much left to discover here, so many secrets buried beneath the ash."

"Secrets like that shrine, perhaps?" I suggested, trying to steer the conversation toward more academic ground.

"Exactly," Dr. Smith said, nodding enthusiastically. "Take this inscription, for example." He leaned in to examine the text, then chuckled. "Ha! It says, '*Venus, bring me a woman with the biggest...*'" He trailed off, winking lewdly at Kerrie before launching into a crude joke about Roman fertility rites.

Kerrie laughed politely, but I could see her discomfort. I exchanged a glance with Niles, who rolled his eyes in silent commiseration.

"Come on," Dr. Smith barked, clapping his hands. "We've got a lot of work to do and not much time to do it. Miles, you and Joe, go check out the Homo Domus. You oughta enjoy that. We'll catch up with ya later."

"Actually, it's—" Niles began, but Dr. Smith had already turned away, leaving him to sigh and adjust his glasses. "Niles," he finished quietly.

I could tell that working with Dr. Smith wouldn't be easy, but I was determined to make the most of this opportunity. Together with Niles, I set off toward the House of the Tragic Poet, eager to uncover the secrets hidden within its walls.

"Are you ready for this?" I asked, trying to lighten the mood.

"Ready as I'll ever be," Niles replied, adjusting his satchel. "Just remember: it's Niles, not Miles."

"Got it," I smiled. "Is he always like this?"

"No, sometimes he's worse."

Dr. Smith eyed me with an unmistakable sneer as we walked into the decrepit old house. "So," he drawled, "you're the Latin geek they saddled me with?" He looked me up and down, taking in my slim frame and tailored clothes before his gaze settled on my wrist, where a rainbow bracelet peeked out from under my sleeve. "Figures," he muttered, shaking his head. "Only faggots and priests learn Latin anyway." I felt my cheeks heat up at his words, but I swallowed my anger, reminding myself that I was here for history, not to make friends.

Niles and I continued to explore the House of the Tragic Poet, our footsteps echoing softly off the ancient walls. As we examined a series of frescoes, Dr. Smith sauntered into the room, smirking as he watched us work side by side.

"Aw, look at you two," he jeered, leaning against a crumbling column. "Miles and Joe, the cutest couple in Pompeii." He looked at Kerrie. "Don't ya think? Aw, what does a woman know?"

Kerrie seethed a little, but held her temper. I was proud of her.

"Actually, I'm not gay," Niles replied, his voice tight with irritation as he brushed a stray lock of hair from his forehead. "And it's *Niles*. Not Miles."

"Whatever," Dr. Smith said dismissively, waving a hand in the air. "Just get back to work." And with that, he turned on his heel and disappeared into another room, leaving Niles and me to exchange weary glances.

"Sorry about him," Niles said, offering me a small smile.

"Don't apologize," I murmured, tracing the lines of a fresco depicting a banquet scene. "It's not your fault he's an ass."

We pressed on, our shared disapproval of Dr. Smith forging a quiet bond between us. As we walked, I marveled at the intricate mosaics beneath our feet, their colors still vibrant after nearly two thousand years. The scent of dust and age filled my nostrils, mingling with the distant tang of the sea.

"Can you imagine what it must have been like to live here?" I mused, running my fingers along the cool stone of a wall adorned with faded frescoes.

"Probably not too different from now," Niles replied, his voice tinged with dry humor. "People are people, no matter when or where they lived."

"True," I conceded, though I couldn't help but think that the inhabitants of ancient Pompeii had faced challenges and joys we could scarcely comprehend.

As we continued to explore, I noticed Niles' eyes lingering on a particular fresco depicting a group of women lounging in a garden. I followed his gaze and noticed that one of the women was depicted with a striking resemblance to Kerrie.

"Hey, isn't that Kerrie?" I asked, pointing at the fresco.

Niles' face grew redder than the fresco itself. "Uh, yeah. I mean, it looks like her."

I chuckled. "Don't worry, I won't tell Dr. Smith you were admiring Kerrie's... fresco."

Niles rolled his eyes, but I could see the corners of his mouth twitching into a smile.

We continued deeper into the house, our footsteps growing slower as we encountered more and more evidence of the tragedy that had befallen Pompeii. A bed, its sheets long since decayed, sat forlornly in one room. In another, a table was still set for a meal, the food and drink that had once graced it long since turned to dust.

As we turned a corner, we were met with a sight that took our breath away. A mural covered an entire wall, its colors still bright and bold despite the passing of centuries. It depicted a scene of such intricate beauty that it was hard to look away. In the center of the mural was a woman, her features delicate and ethereal, surrounded by a riot of flowers and birds. It was as if she had been plucked from the garden itself and set against the wall.

"Wow," I breathed, my hand reaching out to brush the surface of the painting. As we continued our exploration, I tried to put Dr. Smith's comments out of my mind. But his words stung, clinging to me like a stubborn shadow that refused to be banished by the bright Italian sun.

* * *

The sun was relentless, casting the ancient city in a haze of heat as we wandered through the ruins. Our footsteps echoed eerily through the deserted streets, their stones worn smooth by centuries of traffic. I couldn't help but feel a thrill as I walked these narrow lanes, trying to picture what life must have been like in Pompeii all those years ago.

"Over here," Dr. Smith barked, gesturing impatiently towards a large building that loomed ahead of us. "This is the House of the Tragic Poet."

"Wow," Kerrie breathed, her eyes wide with awe as she took in the ornate frescoes and intricate mosaics that adorned the structure's walls. "It's amazing how well-preserved everything is."

"Indeed," I agreed, my heart swelling with pride as I recognized the famous mosaic of a chained dog at the entrance. I couldn't help laughing at it.

"What's so funny?" Kerrie asked.

"This is one of the most iconic images from Pompeii," I explained. "It means 'Beware of the dog.'"

"Sounds like something you'd see on a suburban fence nowadays," Niles chuckled, clearly trying to lighten the mood after our earlier encounter with Dr. Smith. I smiled at him appreciatively, grateful for his efforts.

"Let's move on to the Forum," I suggested, eager to see more of the ancient city. As we made our way through the bustling marketplace, I couldn't help but marvel at the well-preserved remains of the countless shops and stalls that had once lined its perimeter. My mind raced with thoughts of the vibrant colors, tantalizing smells, and lively sounds that must have filled this space in its heyday.

"Over there is the Temple of Jupiter," I said, pointing out the impressive columns that jutted proudly toward the sky. "And that's the Basilica, where legal matters would be resolved."

"Joe, you really know your stuff!" Kerrie exclaimed, her admiration clear in her voice. "You're like a walking encyclopedia of Pompeii."

"Thanks," I replied, feeling a flush of pleasure at the compliment. But as we continued our journey through the city, my thoughts couldn't help but drift to the tragic fate that had befallen its inhabitants.

As we entered the Garden of the Fugitives, I felt my heart grow heavy at the sight of the plaster casts of the people who had been caught in the eruption. Their twisted, contorted forms seemed to cry out in silent agony, forever frozen in their final moments. I could see the fear etched on their faces and imagine the terror that must have gripped them as they realized there was no escape from the deadly cloud that had descended upon them.

"Joe?" Kerrie's gentle touch on my arm jolted me back to the present. "Are you okay?"

My vision blurred with tears as I looked around at the hauntingly beautiful remains of this once-thriving city. "I just can't help but think of all the people who died here," I whispered, my voice choked with emotion. "These people had dreams, hopes, and fears just like us. And in an instant, it was all taken away from them."

"History has a way of reminding us of our own mortality," Niles said softly, his eyes filled with understanding. "But it also teaches us about the resilience of the human spirit. Life goes on, even after tragedy."

I nodded, wiping my eyes as I took a deep breath. This was why I loved history—it connected me to the past, helping me understand not only the triumphs and tragedies of those who came before us, but also the indomitable spirit that unites us all.

As we continued our exploration of the ruins, I was struck by the inscriptions etched into the ancient walls. Many were simple messages, like directions to nearby shops or advertisements for services. But others revealed intimate glimpses into the lives of the people who once called Pompeii home.

"Look at this," I said, pointing to an inscription near the entrance to a house. "It says, 'Lovers, like bees, lead a sweet life.'"

"Leave it to you to find something romantic in all this destruction," Kerrie teased, but her smile didn't quite reach her eyes. I knew she was still shaken by what we had seen earlier.

"Joe, what does that one say?" Niles asked, indicating another inscription further down the wall.

"Ah, that's a little more risqué," I chuckled, translating the Latin. "'I screwed the barmaid.' Seems like some things never change."

"Classic," Niles laughed, and even Kerrie managed a small grin.

"All right, gang, let's call it a day," Dr. Smith announced, wiping the sweat from his brow. "We've got plenty more to see tomorrow, and I don't know about you, but I could use a drink."

"No surprise there," Niles muttered under his breath.

* * *

That evening, we gathered at a small hotel bar in Naples, seeking solace in the camaraderie of our shared experiences. As we sipped our drinks, the atmosphere grew more relaxed, and we began to shed the weight of the day's discoveries. "Tell me more about that inscription you found today, Joe," Kerrie asked as she nursed her glass of wine. "Do you think it was typical for people to express themselves so openly back then?"

"Actually, yes," I replied, my enthusiasm for the subject growing with each word. "The Romans were surprisingly candid about their emotions, desires, and even their bodily functions. Their society, in some ways, was much more open than our own."

"Imagine ol' Cal here fitting in with those loose-lipped Pompeians," Niles mused, stealing a glance at Dr. Smith, who was already on his third drink and growing increasingly boisterous.

"Given how crude some of those inscriptions were," I replied with a grin, thinking of the crude inscriptions we'd seen earlier. "I think he'd fit right in."

As the night wore on and the drinks flowed, the bond between us grew stronger. Despite our differences—and Dr. Smith's questionable antics—we were united by our passion for history and the desire to uncover the secrets of the past.

"Here's to Pompeii," I raised my glass, my eyes meeting those of my companions. "May her stories never be forgotten."

"Cheers!" They echoed, and as our glasses clinked together, I couldn't help but feel grateful for this unique opportunity to explore one of the most fascinating sites in history and do so surrounded by people who shared my love for the ancient world.

Dr. Smith's voice grew louder as he downed another glass of scotch, his cheeks flushed red. He slammed the empty glass on the table, drawing more attention to himself.

"Let me tell you about the time I found the Ark of the Covenant," he slurred, gesturing wildly with his hands. "It was in a hidden chamber beneath the Temple Mount, but the Israeli government didn't want anyone to know about it, so they hushed it up."

"Really?" Kerrie asked skeptically, raising an eyebrow. She glanced at Niles, who sat behind Dr. Smith and shook his head vigorously, mouthing 'no.'

"Absolutely!" Dr. Smith insisted, his words sloppy. "And that's not all. I also found Noah's Ark high up on Mount Ararat. But the Turkish government claimed it was a state secret, so they kept it under wraps." He smugly leaned back in his seat, seemingly very pleased with his fabricated tales.

"Of course," I thought to myself, trying to keep a straight face. "Why wouldn't the governments want to cover up such monumental discoveries?"

Dr. Smith continued to boast about his incredible finds—the Holy Grail in a forgotten catacomb beneath Rome, Cleopatra's tomb in a hidden chamber in Alexandria—each story more outrageous than the last. And at every turn, Niles dutifully shook his head, debunking the lies without saying a word.

Kerrie tried diverting the conversation towards more scholarly topics, but Dr. Smith would have none. Instead, he ordered another round of drinks for the table and clumsily brushed his hand against her thigh, his lecherous gaze fixed on her.

"Doctor Smith," she warned coldly, "don't even think about it."

"Aw, come on, sweetheart," he slurred, attempting to wrap his arm around her shoulders. "Just havin' some fun."

"Fun?" Kerrie hissed, her anger building. "This is not fun. And I am not your sweetheart."

"Lighten up," Dr. Smith replied, oblivious to her discomfort. He leaned in closer, whispering something in her ear that I couldn't hear but could only imagine.

That was the last straw for Kerrie. With a burst of fury, she grabbed her drink and threw it straight into Dr. Smith's face. The ice-cold liquid drenched him, causing him to sputter and choke. Silence fell over the bar as all eyes turned towards our table, watching the scene unfold.

"Get away from me," Kerrie snarled, pushing herself away from the table and storming off.

"Kerrie, wait!" I called after her, but she was already gone.

Dr. Smith wiped wine from his eyes, confusion and embarrassment etched on his face. "What's her problem?" he mumbled, seemingly unaware of his own behavior.

"Her problem?" I said incredulously. "You're the one who crossed the line, Cal."

"Whatever," he grumbled, reaching for another drink. But Niles intervened, snatching the glass away before he could take a sip.

"Maybe you've had enough for tonight," Niles suggested firmly, giving Dr. Smith a pointed look.

"Fine," he muttered, falling back into his seat with a huff.

As I watched the aftermath of the confrontation, I couldn't help but feel a mix of emotions—anger at Dr. Smith's actions, admiration for Kerrie's strength, and concern for how this would affect our team dynamic going forward. Yet, amidst it all, my mind kept drifting back to Pompeii, its ancient walls holding beautiful and tragic secrets, just waiting to be discovered.

* * *

I found Kerrie sitting at the edge of the hotel pool, her legs dangling in the water. She looked up as I approached, eyes red-rimmed from crying. "Hey," I said softly, taking a seat beside her. "You okay?"

"I don't know, Joe," she admitted, her voice catching in her throat. "I think I might have just ruined my entire career."

"Kerrie, come on," I tried to reassure her. "You were defending yourself. That's nothing to be ashamed of."

"Easy for you to say," she muttered, staring down at the water. "You're not the one who just threw a drink in your advisor's face."

"Cal had it coming," I insisted. "And besides, Niles told me that Smith won't even remember what happened by morning."

"Really?" Kerrie glanced over at me, hope flickering in her eyes.

"Trust me," I nodded. "When it comes to Dr. Smith's antics, Niles has seen it all."

Kerrie let out a small laugh, relief washing over her. "Thanks, Joe. I don't know what I'd do without you guys."

"Hey, we're a team," I said, smiling. "We've got your back."

We sat in silence for a moment, enjoying the cool evening breeze and the sound of the water lapping against the pool's edge.

"You know," Kerrie said suddenly, breaking the quiet. "I've been thinking a lot about Pompeii lately. The way the city was frozen in time, preserved by the ash and pumice. It's like a snapshot of history, captured for all time."

"Yeah," I nodded in agreement. "It's an incredible thing to witness."

Kerrie turned to me, her eyes intense. "But what if we could do more than just witness it? What if we could uncover even more than what's been discovered?"

I felt a thrill of excitement surge through me. "You mean, like, new discoveries?"

"Exactly," she said, her gaze never leaving mine. "And not just in Pompeii, but all over the world. I want to be the one to uncover the secrets of the past, to reveal the stories that have been lost to time."

I felt a wave of admiration for my colleague wash over me. This was what made Kerrie so inspiring—her passion for history and her desire to uncover the truth, no matter the cost.

"Count me in," I said, grinning. "Let's make history."

* * *

The next day, the sun blazed down on us as we trudged through the ruins of Pompeii. It was well past 40°C, and every breath felt like inhaling steam. Despite the heat, our team pressed on, eager to uncover more of the city's secrets. We were all hungover, but Dr. Smith was in denial about it. His face was a shade of red that matched his Hawaiian shirt, and beads of sweat formed on his forehead.

"Damn Italians," he grumbled, swiping at his brow with the back of his hand. "Can't make a decent air conditioner to save their lives."

The tension between him and the rest of the team was palpable, but no one wanted to address the elephant in the room. Instead, we focused on our tasks, exploring the remnants of shops and homes that once bustled with life.

"Look at this," Kerrie whispered to me, her fingers tracing the edge of a half-buried urn. "Can you imagine what it must have been like to live here?"

"I can imagine what it was like to die here." I had spent the morning looking at plaster casts of the dead, caught in their final death throes, the screams frozen on their faces. Sometimes I can almost hear their voices," I admitted, my gaze sweeping over the ruins. "I can see them walking through these streets, going about their daily lives. Then, suddenly... boom!"

"Then let's do them justice," she said determinedly. "Let's uncover their stories and share them with the world."

And so we did—or at least tried to—as we dug deeper into Pompeii's past, while avoiding the uncomfortable truth that Cal Smith was becoming more of a hindrance than a help.

Our exploration of the ruins led us to a relatively well-preserved *domus*, which once belonged to a wealthy merchant named Salvius. The structure itself was a testament to his affluence, with ornate frescoes adorning the walls and remnants of intricate mosaics on the floor. Clearly, this man had lived a life of luxury in ancient Pompeii.

"As we walked further into the *domus*, Dr. Smith's attention was suddenly piqued by a peculiar sight. "Well, would you look at that," he muttered, staring at a door that appeared to have been fused shut within the house. The door's wood was charred, contrasting sharply with the otherwise beautifully preserved frescoes surrounding it. Its iron hinges were twisted and warped as if they had been subjected to intense heat.

"Looks like someone didn't want this room to be accessed," Smith mused, stroking his chin thoughtfully. "I wonder what's behind there. Priceless artifacts? Hidden treasure? Maybe just a big dog?"

"More like the bones of one," Niles muttered.

"Dr. Smith, I don't think we should mess with it," Kerrie said cautiously. "It might be dangerous."

"Ah, don't worry your pretty little head about it," he replied dismissively, giving her an exaggerated wink. "I've dealt with worse things than a stuck door in my time. Besides, curiosity is what archaeology's all about."

"Actually, it's about understanding and preserving history," I interjected, unable to resist correcting him. His disdainful gaze settled on me for a moment before he turned back to the door.

"Alright, everyone stand back," he instructed, pulling a crowbar from his bag. "Let's see if we can't crack this mystery wide open."

As he wedged the crowbar between the door and its frame, I couldn't help but wonder what lay behind it. Would we find evidence of Salvius's life and trade? Or would it be another dead end, like so many other rooms we'd explored?

"Any minute now," Dr. Smith grunted, straining against the stubborn door. But despite his efforts, the door refused to budge. Frustration set in, and he resorted to kicking it angrily. Still, it remained firmly shut.

"Damn thing must be cursed," he muttered under his breath, wiping sweat from his brow. "Well, we'll just have to come back later with some heavier equipment. Rome wasn't built in a day, after all."

"Neither was Pompeii," I mumbled to myself, watching as Smith stalked off in search of an easier challenge. In my heart, I couldn't help but feel relieved that the door remained closed. Maybe it held secrets we weren't meant to know.

"Fine, let's try something else," Smith grumbled, rummaging through his bag and pulling out a set of chisels and a hammer. His eyes sparkled with determination as he approached the door again. "If brute force doesn't work, perhaps a little finesse will."

"Be careful not to damage anything," I cautioned, my voice tinged with concern for the ancient artifacts that might be hidden within. "We don't wanna wreck the place."

"Relax, tinkerbell. I know what I'm doing," Smith snapped, clearly irritated by my unsolicited advice. He positioned the chisel against the door's edge and began tapping it gently with the hammer, sending tiny chips of wood flying in every direction.

I stood back, watching him work in uneasy silence. His crude personality and utter disregard for the site's sanctity made me question his qualifications as an archaeologist. But there was no denying his resourcefulness and determination in trying to pry open the mysterious door.

As Smith continued to chip away at the door, I wandered around the room, my eyes drawn to the various frescoes and mosaics adorning the walls. One particular painting caught my attention—a beautifully rendered portrait of a young man, nude but discreetly posed. His dark curls framed a delicate, almost angelic face, his eyes seeming to follow me as I moved about the room.

The emotions that stirred within me were complex: admiration for the artist's skill, envy for the subject's beauty, and a deep, unexplainable longing that sent shivers down my spine. It was as if this stranger from a distant past was reaching out to me, whispering secrets from beyond the veil of time.

"Any luck?" Niles asked, interrupting my reverie.

"Uh, no," I stammered, tearing my gaze away from the painting. "I was just admiring the artwork." I reached out to touch the ancient painting, as if I could feel his face. "He's gorgeous."

"I s'pose," Niles sighed, rolling his eyes, "if you're into that sort of thing. You realize, of course, that he's been dead for two thousand years, right?"

"You're a real buzzkill, Niles," I chuckled.

"Just a realist." Niles replied, his eyes lingering on the portrait for a moment before turning back to Smith. "He's still at it, huh?"

"Yep," I sighed, watching as Smith hammered away with renewed vigor, frustration etching deep lines into his face. "It's like he's trying to conquer the door itself."

"Knowing him, that's exactly what he's doing," Niles said wryly.

As the minutes ticked by, it became increasingly clear that Smith's efforts were in vain. The door remained stubbornly shut, refusing to yield its secrets no matter how hard he tried. But still, he persisted, driven by an insatiable curiosity that bordered on obsession. I decided I had better things to do, so I walked out into the bright sunlight, taking a long swig from my canteen.

Looking down the street, I saw the mountain looming in the distance, a rising mound with a large chunk taken out of it, giving the impression that it was two peaks. What did they ancient Pompeians think, I wondered, when it blew its top that morning back in 79? Surely the ancients knew what a volcano was—Etna was so believed to be the home of Vulcan, their god of fire. Nobody realized that he had a summer home, too.

I could only imagine their shock and surprise.

I paused to watch a team of shirtless men laboring in the hot sun, their sweaty, tanned bodies turning me on. They were clearing away layers of ash and soot compressed over two thousand years. One of them caught me looking and gave me a sly wink. I looked away bashfully, my eyes landing on a shiny object protruding from the ash. I knelt down and tugged on a chain, dislodging a strange-looking amulet. It was a circle with a seven-pointed star, with a green stone set in the center.

I reached down and picked it up.

Big mistake.

Suddenly, I experienced what felt like an electrical shock. My mind exploded into chaos as I felt myself thrown into a void as darkness overcame me....

CHAPTER IV

The dimly lit room swam into focus as my eyes fluttered open. Fear and confusion gripped me; this was not where I had fallen. Just moments ago, it seemed, I was with Dr. Smith's archaeological expedition, exploring the ruins of a villa in Pompeii. Now, I found myself lying on a cold marble floor, my heart pounding in my chest. A cool breeze from the doorway was a dramatic change from the oppressive heat.

"Where am I?" I whispered to myself. I sat up and looked around, feeling a strange sense of *déjà vu*. This room was familiar, yet at the same time, it was strange. Looking up, I saw the fresco on the walls. The image was unmistakable. I had been admiring it just a few moments ago. But something was different. *I'm in the same place*, I realized as I looked around. *But everything is new.* I shook my head in disbelief. Looking over, I saw the stubborn door we had been trying to open. It was ajar now. Judging from the darkness within, it led to a windowless room that would probably be intact when Cal finally got it open.

Suddenly I heard paws scampering across the marble floor, and a massive mastiff bounded over and knocked me to the floor. I was expecting this Baskervillian hound to bite my face off, but he slid his warm, wet tongue across my face instead. "Hey there, Doggo," I said, trying to keep my voice steady despite my mounting anxiety. "You're a good boy, aren't ya?" As I petted the dog, reality still refused to sink in. There was no way this could possibly be happening. My mind raced, searching for explanations. Was this some elaborate prank? Or perhaps I'd been drugged and kidnapped by one of Dr. Smith's rivals? No, I had passed out from the heat and had a fever dream... right?

"Where am I, boy?" I asked the dog, half hoping for an intelligent response, but the beast had never heard English before. Instead, the mastiff wagged its tail and panted happily, clearly enjoying the attention. "All right then," I muttered under my breath, realizing that talking to a dog wasn't going to get me any answers. I decided it was time to step outside and see if I could figure out what was going on.

"Hello?" I asked the first person I saw. "Can you help me...."

"*Non intellego*," the stranger shrugged. "*Non loquor lingua tua.*"

I had to take a moment to parse that out. *I don't understand*, he was saying, *I don't speak your language*—in Latin!

So I asked again. "*Ubi sum?*" (Where am I?)

The stranger stared at me curiously, and for the first time, I noticed that the clothes I was wearing were gone. I was now dressed in a light tunic over a loincloth, the garb of a pauper. "Where do you think you are, young man?" he replied in a crude Latin dialect, raising an eyebrow. "This is Pompeii, of course."

"Right, Pompeii," I said. The big mountain made it kind of obvious. "Of course. *Quid est hodie?*" (What day is this?)

"*Et iides Augusta.*" The ides of August. August 13th.

"*Quid est annus?*" I asked him. (What year is it?)

The man shook his head. "Perhaps you shouldn't drink so much wine, friend. Begone, I have no time for your nonsense."

I asked another passerby, a woman carrying a basket of fruit.

"Year? What an odd question." She looked puzzled before walking away, trying to decide if I was a madman or just an idiot.

"Fuck you, bitch," I grumbled, not that anyone understood what I was saying. English didn't exist yet. As I walked through the streets, I marveled at the architectural wonders surrounding me. I passed bustling bathhouses, colorful marketplaces, and even a beautifully preserved amphitheater. But despite the awe-inspiring sights, my mind was consumed by one thought: how was all this possible?

"Hey!" a voice shouted in Latin, snapping me out of my reverie. "Watch where you're going!"

"I'm so, so sorry," I apologized, realizing I had almost bumped into a young girl carrying a tray of delicate pottery.

"Be more careful next time," she warned, her eyes narrowing as she scrutinized me. "You don't look like you're from around here."

"Uh, no," I admitted. "I'm not."

"Strange clothes, strange accent," she observed, not unkindly. "Yet you speak like a scholar. You must have quite a story."

"More than you know," I muttered, wondering if I could ever share it with anyone who would believe me.

"Welcome to Pompeii," she said, flashing a warm smile before continuing on her way.

I thought of Dr. Clarke, my iron-fisted high school Latin teacher. Her face was stern and her gaze fiery as she paced between two wooden desks, flipping a long pointer in her hands like a whip. She had no patience for mistakes or laziness, and she made sure we knew every declension and conjugation by heart. We would sit for hours at the same wooden desk, parsing verbs until they were second nature to us; then, she would make us recite passages from Caesar and Cicero until we could pronounce every syllable with a perfect accent. Her pen scratched across the paper as she marked our papers with red ink until they looked like they had been dipped in blood. We all feared and respected her. Somewhere, I figured, she was laughing at me. Then I realized that she hadn't been born yet.

Taking a deep breath, I turned a corner and looked at the mountain. Vesuvius stood tall and proud over the city. My heart skipped a beat as I saw the lush green slopes of the pristine, unblemished peak, a stark contrast to the mountain I remembered that had a big bite taken out of it. The ancient Vesuvius was a tapered peak that loomed large and powerful, yet deceivingly tranquil, like a sleeping giant unaware of its own power, a power it would soon unleash. But how soon?

"Excuse me, sir," I asked a passing merchant, trying to keep my tone casual despite the urgency I felt. "What year is this?"

"Year?" he replied, looking at me as if I'd lost my mind. "How do you not know what year it is?"

"Sorry, I've been traveling for a while and just arrived in Pompeii," I lied, hoping my Latin would pass. "I must have lost track of time."

"I'll say. Begone, beggar, I have no time for you." he shook his head and turned up his nose before continuing on his way.

"Thanks," I muttered, racking my brain for any information that might help me pinpoint the exact date. If only I'd paid more attention in my Roman history classes!

"Are you lost, stranger?" a kindly old woman asked, noticing my bewildered expression.

"Sort of," I admitted. "I'm trying to figure out what year it is."

"Ah, young people these days," she chuckled. "Always so preoccupied with the future! You should enjoy the present, my dear. Life in Pompeii is a gift."

"Thank you," I said, taking her words to heart as I looked around at the vibrant city that would soon be lost to history. "You're right. I should appreciate what I have while I'm here."

"Indeed," she agreed, patting my arm gently before shuffling away.

As I continued wandering through Pompeii streets, I tried to piece together the puzzle of my situation. Was the eruption days, months, or even years away? And, more importantly, how could I find a way back to my own time before it was too late?

I looked around, taking in the sights and sounds of ancient Pompeii. The vibrant colors of frescoes adorned the walls of buildings, and the chatter of people going about their daily lives filled my ears. It was mesmerizing and terrifying at once, knowing that this thriving city would be buried under volcanic ash in the near future.

Just then the gods decided to do me a solid. A sheet of paper adrift on the wind landed on my feet. It was the *Acta Diurna*, the newspaper of the Roman Empire. I barely caught a glimpse at the date before its owner came along and snatched it away. It was a long string of Roman numerals I barely had time to translate: DC-

CCXXXI. That told me that the year was 831 A.U.C., according to the *ab urbe condita* calendar the Empire used. It was based on the founding of Rome in… shit! When was that? *Of all the stupid, trivial facts to forget!*

All I knew was that it was before 79 C.E. The mountain told me that. It was a different Vesuvius from the one I had seen minutes before, centuries later. It rose to a smooth, flattened plateau as opposed to the shattered remnant with a giant hole blasted in its side. The giant was sleeping, but it was going to wake up. But would it be today? Tomorrow? Next week? Next year…?

"Hey! You there!" a gruff voice called out to me, snapping me back to reality. I turned to see a burly man with a bald head and a thick beard standing in the doorway of a nearby building. He was dressed in rough, simple clothing and had the air of someone who was used to being in charge. "Are you the new *exoletus?*" he asked, eyeing me up and down. "You're late."

"*Exoletus?*" I stammered, trying to figure out what he meant. It was an obscure word, but an *exoletus* was… a male prostitute! What had I gotten myself into?

"You heard me," he barked, waving me over impatiently. "Come on, I don't have all day. Get inside."

I hesitated, unsure of what to do. I had never been mistaken for a prostitute before, but I knew I didn't want to be involved in anything unsavory. I looked around, hoping to find a way out of the situation, but it seemed that all eyes were on me. Taking a deep breath, I stepped forward, trying to keep a straight face as I approached the burly man. "I'm sorry, but you've got the wrong person," I said, hoping to convince him to let me go.

But he wasn't buying it. "Don't play dumb with me, boy," he growled, grabbing me by the arm and pulling me into the building. "The master is waiting for you."

I struggled against his grip, but it was no use. He was too strong for me. I felt a sense of panic rising in my chest as he dragged me deeper into the building, the sounds of the street fading away behind us.

"Listen up because I won't repeat myself," Gaius barked, leading me through a narrow hallway. "Your job is to please our clients. Do whatever they want—within reason, of course. Any complaints, you'll answer to me. Understand?"

"Yes, sir," I replied hesitantly, realizing that playing along might be my best chance of figuring out how to get out of this mess.

"Good," Gaius grunted, pushing open the door to reveal a small room where three young men lounged on couches, looking bored. "These are your fellow *exoleti*: Petrus, Tiberius, and Antonius. They'll show you the ropes."

"So this is a wet dream," I noted, thinking out loud in my mother tongue while looking over the three gods who stood over me.

Petrus looked down at me, his brow furrowed. "What language is that?"

"Sounds like Celtic," Antonius said. "I've heard they are insatiable." He rose from his seat and tugged away his loincloth to let his flag fly. "We'll just have to see about that, won't we?"

As they rose from their seats, wearing only skimpy loincloths, I felt a familiar stirring in my crotch. Petrus grabbed at my tunic and tore it away, yanking away the loincloth beneath so that my erect penis sprang to attention. Petrus grinned a lascivious grin. "I like a man who's prepared." He pulled at his loincloth and it fell away. "I am called Petrus." I could see why; he was as hard as a rock, from his solid chest to his erect phallus. "Your first lesson will be giving oral service."

I laughed. "Lesson? I need no lesson!" I dropped to my knees and took his shaft all the way down my throat, sending ripples of ecstasy through Petrus. What can I say? I know how to give legendary blow jobs.

"By the gods!" Petrus gasped. "You should be teaching us! Venus herself must have taught you how to do that!"

"She's not my type, actually," I smirked.

Antonius approached me next, stroking my buttock with an approving smile and smearing olive oil onto my anus. "Can you take it through the back?" he purred into my ear as he pressed himself into me. Soon he was pounding me with all his might while I cried out in delight. "*Oh yes!*" I cried out in English, unable to contain my enthusiasm any longer. "*Oh god, yes!*"

Antonius paused. "Then it's true what they say about Celts?" Antonius asked, his brow furrowed in confusion. "Whatever you said, it certainly sounds... passionate."

"Indeed," I agreed, forcing a laugh and hoping they'd let the matter drop. And much to my relief, they did—for now, at least. But I couldn't shake the feeling that I was playing a dangerous game that could end badly if I wasn't careful. "Now, please finish what you were doing."

Antonius grinned and whispered in my ear. "I already have."

"You service well," Tiberius observed. "But not all of our clients seek a dominant experience. There are those who prefer to submit." He commanded me to lie down, lean over me, and wrap his mouth around my throbbing manhood. I wasn't sure if he was testing my endurance or just how I tasted. I was so aroused I was probably about to erupt like Vesuvius.

"Let me show you something," I told him. "Lie down next to me and do that, but with your head the other way." He figured out what I was talking about and was pleased to discover that it was a more comfortable angle. But he didn't expect me to lean over and take him into my mouth, too.

Petrus and Antonius watched in shock. "Do you see that, Petrus?" Antonius gasped. "He gives and receives at the same time!"

"Surely we have met our match, my brothers," Petrus nodded. "It's so simple! I never realized two bodies fit together like that!"

"I see it!" Antonius nodded. "Who is this man of so many talents?"

I sat up long enough to answer. "It's called sixty-nining."

Antonious looked at me strangely, then counted on his fingers. "Why?"

Oops. It suddenly dawned on me that 6 and 9, like all the other Arabic numerals (which are actually Hindu), wouldn't even exist for another five hundred years. Somehow, LXIX-ing doesn't quite get the idea across.

"Never mind. It's just fun."

"I want to try!" Antonius had Petrus lie down, looking over at me and repeating the same motions. They caught on quickly.

The *exoleti* exchanged glances before nodding in agreement, a wicked smile spreading across each of their faces. And so, we embarked on a night of unbridled passion, exploring the limits of our desire in ways that would make even the most jaded Roman blush. As they took turns pleasuring me in increasingly inventive ways, I lost myself in ecstasy, my thoughts of escape fading into the background.

As the night wore on and the intensity of our encounters reached dizzying new heights, I knew I had to find a way out of this nightmare—dream or not—before it consumed me entirely.

* * *

I lay on the soft cushions, the scent of perfumed oils lingering in the air. My body felt like it had been pushed to its limits and beyond, but there was a strange sense of satisfaction, too. As I caught my breath, trying to make sense of the whirlwind of events that had brought me here, I couldn't help but wonder if this were all just some bizarre dream. Perhaps I'd wake up any moment now, back in my own bed, in my own time. "Hey," I said, clearing my throat as the three exhausted *exoleti* sprawled around me began to stir. "Anybody have a cigarette?"

They looked at me blankly, clearly not understanding the joke. I sighed inwardly, realizing I probably should've expected that. Just as well; I don't smoke anyway.

"By the gods," Petrus panted, too spent to move a muscle. "Is there no end to your appetite?"

"None that I know of," I smirked. "I'm up for more anytime you're ready, boys."

"You will certainly be popular with the clients," Tiberius noted.

"Should we be nervous?" Antonius asked. "He could replace us all with his stamina."

"Then who would take care of me?" I smiled. "Don't worry, your jobs are all safe."

"I need sleep," Petrus groaned. "Maybe then I can 'train' you some more."

"I certainly look forward to that," I smiled.

"Yes," Tiberius smiled. "Then you can train us."

"I look forward to that, too. I'm sure there is much that I can teach you."

Meanwhile, at Salvius Marcellus's villa, Gaius anxiously approached his master with news of the new arrival at Homo Domus. "*Dominus* Salvius," he began hesitantly, "I wanted to let you know that the new slave you sent us for training this morning is performing *exceptionally* well."

"That is good to—" Salvius furrowed his brow, confusion etched across his face. "Wait, what? New slave, you say? I haven't purchased a new slave."

Gaius blinked, taken aback by Salvius's response. "But—he's at the Domus being trained."

"By the gods!" Salvius exclaimed, worry creeping into his voice. "We need to correct this immediately! There could be serious legal repercussions if we're discovered harboring someone who doesn't belong to us!"

"Of course, *dominus*," Gaius replied, bowing his head before hurrying alongside Salvius as they made their way back to Homo Domus.

Back in the chamber where I'd spent the night in debauchery, I idly traced patterns on the elaborate mosaic floor with my fingertips, trying to piece together what I knew of ancient Pompeii in an attempt to understand my predicament. My mind raced with questions, fears, and doubts. If this wasn't a dream, how had I ended up here? Was there any way to get back to my own time?

The door burst open, and Salvius stormed in, Gaius following closely behind. "What is the meaning of this?" Salvius demanded, his eyes sweeping over the scene with a mix of confusion and anger.

"Uh, hi," I said weakly, pushing myself into a sitting position and desperately hoping that this man—whoever he was—could somehow help me make sense of it all.

"Stop right there!" Salvius commanded, holding up a hand. "Who are you, and what are you doing in my establishment?"

I decided it best to cooperate for the moment. "I, uh... I'm not entirely sure how I got here."

"Neither am I," Salvius grumbled, turning to Gaius with a glare. "You said I sent him here?"

Gaius nodded nervously, wringing his hands. "That's what I thought, *dominus*. He seemed so sure of himself, so... experienced."

"Experienced?" I snorted involuntarily, then immediately regretted it as both men turned their attention back to me. "Sorry," I mumbled, trying to regain some semblance of composure. "Look, I don't know what's going on or how I ended up here, but I promise you, I'm not trying to cause any trouble."

"Very well," Salvius said after a moment's consideration, his tone softening somewhat. "We'll get to the bottom of this. But first, let's get you cleaned up and properly dressed. Please, come with me to my home."

"Thanks," I said gratefully, feeling a flicker of hope that maybe, just maybe, I'd found an ally in this strange and bewildering world.

* * *

"*Mea culpa!*" Salvius said earnestly, his deep brown eyes filled with genuine remorse. "*Mea culpa! Mea maxima culpa!* I cannot apologize enough for this misunderstanding. I assure you, had I known of your true nature and intentions, I would never have allowed Gaius to bring you here."

"*Ego te absolvo*," I said with a casual shrug, secretly marveling at the way the sunlight streaming through the open window caught the intricate carvings on the wall. "To be honest, I find your staff to be very, uh, accommodating. I almost feel like I should pay for the service. Like I said before, it was just an... average Saturday night for me. Besides, I've always been one to roll with the punches." I had no idea how to teach an ancient Roman to pronounce a J sound, so I romanized my name on the fly. "I am Iosephus Andrius, a traveling historian. You may call me Io."

"Ah, a man of learning," Salvius replied, a hint of admiration creeping into his voice. "I should have known!" My school-taught Latin, perfect and precise, had him thinking I was a sage. "I can tell by the way you speak so perfectly and precisely." *Yeah, thanks, Dr. Clarke.* "Well then, my dear Io, as a token of my goodwill and in the hopes of making amends for our unfortunate first encounter, allow me to extend an invitation to my home. You shall be an honored guest, and I'm sure we'll have much to discuss."

"Thank you, Salvius," I said, touched by his generosity and eager to learn more about this strange old world I found myself in. "I'd be honored to accept your invitation."

"Excellent," he said, clapping his hands together briskly. "Marcus!" he called out, and a young man with curly brown hair and deep brown eyes appeared at the door. "This is my servant, Marcus. He will see to your every need while you're under my roof."

My eyes widened in shock as recognition hit me like a ton of bricks. Of course, I knew him! He was the man from the painting, the one I had seen in the ruins just before I fainted and found myself here, now. It must be him—there was no mistaking it. My heart pounded furiously as I realized who he was.

"*Salve, dominus,*" Marcus said, bowing low to me. As he straightened, I couldn't help noticing the way his tunic clung to his lean, muscular frame. He was even more beautiful in the flesh. He noticed my stupor and his brow creased. "Are you all right, *dominus?*"

"S-S-*Salve*, Marcus," I replied, feeling a warm flush creep up my neck as our eyes met, and I quickly looked away. "I welcome your assistance, and your friendship."

"Of course, *dominus,*" he said with a shy smile. "If you'll follow me, I'll show you to your quarters."

As we made our way through the bustling streets of Pompeii, I couldn't help but feel a strange mix of awe and trepidation. Everywhere I looked, there were reminders of the vibrant, thriving city that had once stood here—and the terrible fate that awaited it.

"Marcus," I ventured hesitantly, my historian's curiosity getting the better of me, "do you know anything about...Vesuvius?"

Marcus up at the looming mountain that dominated the horizon. "Well, it's said to have once been the home of the god Vulcan in ancient times, but other than that... it's just a mountain. Vulcan lives on Etna now. Though his presence can still be felt from the mountain; in his benevolence, he warms us in winter."

"Right," I murmured, feeling a chill run down my spine despite the warmth of the sun on my face. Etna was a more active volcano. Vesuvius had never erupted in human memory. At least not these humans' memory. "Just a mountain."

"Is something wrong, *dominus?*" Marcus asked, his brow furrowed in concern.

"No, nothing at all," I reassured him, forcing a smile. "I'm just... still adjusting to everything, I suppose. I, uh, haven't eaten that well in a while."

"You shall eat well tonight at my master's table. But I sense more than that. You seem to fear the mountain. Your voice trembles when you talk about it." He looked at me with deep brown eyes. "There is something unusual about you, Iosephus. You aren't from this place, or any place I know. But I see great wisdom in your eyes." He put a hand to my forearm. His touch was warm and inviting. "But most of all, you have the eyes of someone who is lost."

"You've no idea how lost I am," I frowned.

Marcus smiled and put a reassuring hand on my shoulder. "You are among friends here."

CHAPTER V

As I explored Salvius's villa, I was struck by the opulence that surrounded me. The walls were adorned with intricate frescoes depicting scenes of gods and goddesses while mosaic floors sparkled beneath our feet. I had seen such artwork in museums and textbooks, but seeing them here, in their original context, was a surreal experience.

"Welcome to our home, Iosephus," Salvius greeted warmly, leading me into the main dining area. There, I met his elegant wife, Livia, who possessed an air of serene refinement. Her dark hair was arranged in an elaborate updo, and her eyes held a glint of curiosity as she regarded me.

"Salvius has told me much about you, Iosephus," she said graciously, extending a hand for me to kiss. "It is a pleasure to finally meet you."

"Likewise, *domina*," I replied, bowing over her hand. My nerves were on edge, but maintaining my manners felt like a lifeline to some semblance of normalcy.

"And this is my son Quintus!" Salvius exclaimed as a young man entered the room, his features strikingly resembling his father's. His eyes were lively with interest as he assessed me, clearly intrigued by the stranger in his home. "Quintus, this is Iosephus Andrius, a historian from... Alexandria, you say?"

"Yes," I nodded. "Alexandria." It was probably the only honest answer I could give; I *was* born in Alexandria. The one in Minnesota, which hadn't even been built yet.

"*Salve*, Iosephus," Quintus greeted, offering a firm handshake. "I look forward to hearing more about your travels."

"*Salve*, Quintus," I responded, returning the gesture. "I'm eager to share what I know."

As we took our places at the table, I couldn't help but notice the large, friendly mastiff that had been my initial companion in this strange new world. He padded over and sat obediently at Salvius's side, wagging his tail as he looked up at his master.

"Ah, Iosephus," Salvius chuckled, noticing my attention on the dog, "I see you've already met Canno."

"Indeed," I said, smiling down at the dog. "He was the first friendly face I encountered here. He's a good boy."

"Indeed he is," Livia added with a smile. "Canno is the most loyal companion one could ask for."

As the meal began, I found myself faced with a veritable feast of unfamiliar foods. There were dormice cooked in honey and poppy seeds, peacock tongues, and even roasted flamingo, delicacies I had never imagined eating. Trying to ignore my initial hesitation, I sampled each dish, finding that some were surprisingly delicious while others required an acquired taste.

"Have you ever tried garum, Iosephus?" Quintus asked, gesturing to a small jar of the pungent, fermented fish sauce that Romans often used as a condiment.

"Uh, no, I haven't," I admitted, fighting the urge to wrinkle my nose at the strong aroma.

"Give it a try," Livia encouraged. "It enhances the flavor of nearly every dish."

Nodding hesitantly, I drizzled a small amount of the sauce onto my plate and tentatively tasted it. To my surprise, it did indeed add a savory depth to the food, despite its off-putting scent.

"Delicious," I murmured, earning nods from my hosts.

Perhaps the most challenging aspect of the dinner was adjusting to the Roman custom of eating while reclining on one's side. Propped up on my left elbow, I struggled to find a comfortable position and maintain my balance as I reached for various dishes. Salvius and his family, however, seemed completely at ease with the practice, gracefully navigating their meal without so much as a dropped morsel.

When in Pompeii, I guess....

"Is this your first time eating in such a manner, Iosephus?" Livia inquired, noticing my awkwardness.

"Indeed, *domina*," I confessed. "It's quite different from what I'm used to."

"Ah, well," she said kindly, "you'll grow accustomed to it with time. It is simply the way of our people."

As we continued to eat and converse, I found myself absorbing details of life in ancient Pompeii through their stories and experiences. In this strange new world, I was grateful for the warmth and hospitality of the Marcellus family, even as the specter of Vesuvius loomed in the back of my mind. For now, though, I would savor the present, taking comfort in the company of newfound friends and the loyal presence of Canno by my side.

Just as I was beginning to feel more at ease, the front door swung open, and a jovial man in his forties entered the room. His dark eyes sparkled with excitement, and he greeted Salvius with a warm embrace.

"Ah, Nuntius! Welcome, friend!" Salvius exclaimed, gesturing for him to join us at the table. "This is our new acquaintance, Iosephus Andrius—or Io, for short."

"*Salve*, Io," Nuntius said with a friendly grin, extending his hand to me. "I have heard much about you already."

"*Salve*, Nuntius," I replied, shaking his hand firmly. "It's a pleasure to meet you."

As we continued our meal, Nuntius regaled us with tales of his recent travels and news from around the empire. At one point, he mentioned the Roman victory at Masada, describing the triumphant conquest of the Judean fortress. It was my first clue toward figuring out the date. The siege of Masada took place between 73 and 74 C.E. "Masada was a tragic event, though, wasn't it?" I interjected before I could help myself. "Most of the Judeans chose to take their own lives rather than be captured by the Romans."

A sudden hush fell over the table, as if I'd let out a really loud fart, and I instantly regretted my words. Nuntius blinked in surprise while Salvius and Livia exchanged concerned glances. Quintus stared at me, wide-eyed.

"Uh, I mean… that's what I've heard," I stammered, feeling my cheeks grow hot. "I apologize if I misspoke."

"No, no, you're quite right," Nuntius said slowly, eyeing me with curiosity. "It's just that... such information hasn't been widely circulated. Your knowledge of current events is impressive, Io."

One man's history, I pondered, is another man's current events. "Thank you," I mumbled, trying to suppress my embarrassment. I decided to steer the conversation toward safer territory. "I have learned much in my travels." Maybe I could learn more from Nuntius. "So, Nuntius, what other news can you share from the empire?"

"Ah, well," he began, taking a sip of wine. "Did you know that our esteemed Emperor Vespasian has now been on the throne for nine years? Such stability after the tumultuous year of the four emperors."

"Nine years?" I echoed, my mind racing as I did the mental calculations. *Bingo!* Vespasian's reign began in 69 C.E., the year of the four emperors, and ended with his death in June 79 C.E. Nine years later meant it was now 78 C.E. August 13th, 78 C.E.—the eruption was thirteen months away.

"Indeed," Salvius nodded, seemingly unaware of my internal turmoil. "His rule has brought many improvements to the empire—the construction of the Flavian Amphitheatre and the establishment of a stable currency, to name just a few."

"The amphitheater is impressive," Nuntius noted. "It's not as large as the Circus Maximus, but it's an architectural wonder."

I smirked at the thought that just the day before, I had toured the ruins of the Flavian Amphitheatre, now just called the Colosseum. Then I realized it was actually 1,940 years from now. It suddenly dawned on me that I had to be careful how I changed history. What if I created a grandfather paradox and prevented myself from being born? Just thinking about it was giving me a headache.

As they continued discussing the highlights of Vespasian's reign, a growing sense of dread settled in my chest. I was trapped in Pompeii with no way of returning to my own time, and the deadly eruption of Vesuvius was now just a little more than a year away.

* * *

As I lay down on the soft cushion in the guest room, still feeling the weight of the revelation that Vesuvius would erupt in just over a year, my thoughts were a maelstrom of fear and uncertainty. How could I survive in this ancient world, with all its dangers and unfamiliar customs? My heart raced as I thought about what was to come.

My thoughts were interrupted as the door creaked open, revealing Marcus's silhouette. He hesitated for a moment before entering the room, his eyes locked on mine.

"Marcus," I whispered, unsure of what he wanted. "What are you doing here?"

"I... I heard your conversation at dinner," he confessed, his voice trembling. "You... you sounded so wise, so knowledgeable. I thought perhaps you could use some comfort."

Slowly, he stepped further into the room, allowing the dim light from the oil lamp to reveal his body, now stripped of clothing. He stood there, vulnerable and exposed yet still strong and determined.

"Are you offering yourself to me?" I asked, my voice barely above a whisper.

"Yes," he replied, his cheeks flushing. "If you'll have me."

In that instant, I saw not the trained submissive that Marcus had been molded into by his experiences, but a man who desired connection and equality. It stirred something within me, igniting a spark that had been dormant during my encounters at the brothel.

"Come here," I said softly, reaching out to him.

He approached hesitantly at first, but as our fingers touched, he seemed to gain confidence. We locked eyes, and I pulled him close, our bodies pressed against each other.

"Let me show you something different," I murmured as I brushed a strand of hair from his face.

Our lips met, and the intimacy of the kiss sent shivers down my spine. This wasn't the wild, unrestrained passion of the *exoleti*, but something tender and genuine. I guided him onto the bed, our bodies entwined as we explored each other with a delicate curiosity, kissing passionately.

"Can I do this?" Marcus asked, his voice shaky as he touched me in ways he had never been allowed to before.

"Of course," I whispered, my heart swelling at the thought of sharing this new experience with him. "We're equals here."

As we made love, I reveled in the intimacy and connection that had been so absent during my earlier escapades. Marcus seemed to bloom with every caress and kiss, embracing the unfamiliar role of an equal partner. Our bodies moved in harmony, and for a moment, I forgot about the looming threat of Vesuvius.

Afterward, as we lay wrapped in each other's arms, I marveled at how quickly my feelings for Marcus had grown. The world outside might be dangerous and uncertain, but here, in this quiet room, I had found something worth fighting for.

"Thank you," Marcus murmured, his eyes welling up with unshed tears.

"Thank you, too," I replied, my own emotions threatening to spill over. "For showing me what true connection can feel like."

As we drifted off to sleep, I clung to the warmth of Marcus's body and the knowledge that, even in this foreign land, I had found someone who could understand and care for me. The future may be uncertain, but as long as we had each other, perhaps there was still hope.

* * *

The first light of dawn crept through the window, casting a warm glow on Marcus's slumbering face. As I stared at him, taking in his chest's gentle rise and fall, reality washed over me like a tidal wave.

This was not a dream—I was still trapped in ancient Pompeii, with no way to return home.

My breath hitched as the weight of my situation bore down on me. The faces of my friends and family flashed through my mind, their smiles and laughter growing more distant with each passing moment. A cold fear gripped my heart, and tears welled up in my eyes.

"Marcus," I choked out, my voice barely a whisper. "I need you."

He stirred in my arms, blinking sleepily at me. "Io? What's wrong?"

I tried to speak, but the words caught in my throat. How could I explain everything that had happened—the time travel, the impending eruption of Vesuvius and destruction of Pompeii and Herculaneum—without sounding insane?

"Hey," he murmured, cupping my cheek with one hand. "Talk to me."

"Promise me something," I said instead, my voice quivering. "No matter what happens, please... stay by my side."

"Of course," he assured me, his brow furrowing with concern. "But why are you so afraid?"

"Because..." I hesitated, searching for the right words. "Because there are things in this world we cannot control. And sometimes, it feels like those things will swallow us whole."

"Ah," Marcus nodded, his expression softening. "But that is why we must cling to what we can control—our love, our loyalty, our friendships. Those things can anchor us in the storm."

"Thank you," I whispered, burying my face in his shoulder as sobs wracked my body. He held me close, his strong arms a comforting embrace.

"Come," he said, gently wiping away my tears after a while. "Let us start the day together. Perhaps we can find some solace in the simple pleasures of life."

We rose from the bed and dressed, Marcus leading me through the bustling streets of Pompeii. As we walked, I marveled at the vivid colors of the frescoes that adorned the walls and the intricate mosaics beneath our feet. The air was thick with the scent of fresh bread and roasting meats, and the clamor of merchants hawking their wares filled my ears.

"Over there," he gestured toward a nearby bakery, "is where we can purchase one of Pompeii's finest honey cakes—a treat fit for the gods themselves."

As we continued on, Marcus regaled me with tales of everyday life in Pompeii, his enthusiasm infectious. In those moments, I found a small measure of peace, a reminder that even in the darkest times, there were still glimmers of light.

Yet, as we turned a corner and caught sight of Vesuvius looming ominously in the distance, I couldn't help but shudder. The people of Pompeii went about their lives, unaware of the catastrophe that would soon befall them. And though I still had no way of returning home, I knew that I would do everything in my power to protect those I had come to care for—Marcus, Salvius, and everyone else who had shown me kindness in this strange new world.

"Marcus," I said softly, clutching his hand tightly. "No matter what the future holds, I promise that I will always fight for you—for us."

"Likewise," he replied, giving my hand a reassuring squeeze. And as we stood side by side, I took solace in the knowledge that we would never be alone, even in the face of the unknown.

* * *

I arrived home to Domus Marcelli in a swirl of dust, the late afternoon sun filtering through the courtyard like golden fingers. The familiar sight of Marcus greeted me as I walked through the door. He bowed formally, his long curly hair, brown eyes, and lean frame a reminder of the sweet boy he had been when I had first arrived at Domus Marcelli as a young man.

"Welcome home, dominus," Marcus said, his voice low and steady.

"Please don't call me that," I told him gently. "I'm not your master."

"Have I offended you…?"

"No, not at all. I would just rather be your friend than your master. Please, call me Io."

Marcus smiled. "I've never had a 'friend' before."

"Never? Not even when you were a boy?"

Marcus frowned. "My parents had their own idea of who I should be," he said sadly. "They wanted me to be a gladiator. I trained for it my entire childhood." That explained why Marcus had such a smoking hot body. "When the time came, I disappointed them because I'm not a fighter. I never have been."

"I see," I nodded. "Make love, not war."

"Yes," Marcus smiled. "I want to make love… with you, Io."

I leaned in and kissed him gently. His lips were full and soft, and it felt good to press mine against them. His kiss wasn't exactly sweet; remember, they used urine to brush their teeth. But for a man as hot as Marcus, I could even grow to like the taste.

Soon my tongue was exploring his mouth, and I was easing him back on the mattress of my bed. The sun was just beginning to dip below the horizon, casting a warm orange glow over the courtyard. With each step I took, I raised a cloud of dust that sparkled in the fading light and settled back into the crevices between the cracked paving stones. A strange sense of calm descended on me as I stepped through the archway and into the villa, and for the first time in months, my heart felt full.

I thanked Marcus as I stepped through the villa, feeling the familiar creaking of the floorboards and the smell of cedar in the air. I had missed this place, and the feeling of coming home.

Marcus opened my chamber door and gestured for me to enter first. The room was exactly as I remembered it, with a large bed covered in a soft quilt, a fireplace glowing embers, and a desk covered in papers and books.

Marcus stepped inside as I looked around, my eyes lingering on the paintings of my beloved family that hung on the walls.

"Please, let me help you undress," Marcus asked quietly.

That would be such a turn-on. I nodded silently, my throat too tight for words. My hands trembled slightly as Marcus helped me out of my clothes, carefully peeling away the fabric until I stood exposed and vulnerable before him. With a tug, his loincloth fell away and his penis sprang to attention. Without speaking a word, I sank to one knee to genuflect before him, opening my mouth and taking his salty penis into my mouth, peeling back the foreskin to give the head a gentle kiss.

"I should be the one servicing you," Marcus gasped, despite the waves of ecstasy he was feeling.

I stood up and kissed him again. "Who says we can't do both?" I laid him back on the bed and laid down opposite him, taking his manhood into my mouth as he went to work on mine. He fell back away from me as I felt the wave begin to swell within him. His chest heaved up and down as it rose to a crescendo, then with a grunt he shot a huge load into my mouth. As I swirled his semen around in my mouth, I realized that Marcus was vegan.

I can taste when a guy is vegetarian by the taste of his cum.

Marcus leaned over and wrapped his lips around my penis again, and within a minute I was shooting my load into his mouth. He swallowed it with a smile, even though it probably doesn't taste as good as his does.

The air was cool against my skin, but Marcus' gaze felt like a warm embrace, making me feel safe and cherished. He then joined me on the bed, curling himself around my body like a shield. His warmth surrounded me like a cocoon, seeping into my being and calming me.

I nestled into his embrace as the gentle heat of the crackling fire caressed my face. The chirping of crickets outside in the tranquil night lulled us to sleep, and for the first time since I'd arrived, I felt a true sense of peace. Even if I could find a way back home, part of me didn't want to leave this place. Domus Marcelli was now my home away from home—a sanctuary that I could always rely on.

Suddenly the prospect of being trapped in time here didn't seem so bad… except for that damned volcano looming over everything like a ticking time bomb.

CHAPTER VI

Three months had passed since my arrival in ancient Pompeii, and I was beginning to adjust to my new normal. It was November and the days were growing shorter, the air cooler. It was a far cry from the world I'd left behind, but in many ways, it felt like home. My name now was Iosephus Andrius, a Romanized version of my own, and my many friends called me Io.

My daily routine started with a cup of posca, a sour wine that was popular among the locals. Then, I would stroll through the streets, offering counsel to those who sought it.

I owed much of my acclimation to Marcus, the dark-haired young man who had taken me under his wing. He taught me the social and cultural norms of this time, guiding me through the intricacies of life in ancient Rome. Together, we navigated the bustling marketplace, the crowded bathhouses, and the raucous taverns. He showed me how to properly wear a toga, how to address my elders, and even how to appreciate the finer points of gladiatorial combat.

The first thing I had to re-learn was how to shake hands with people. They grasped each other's forearm's instead, just below the elbow. The next thing I learned is that when your Latin is as perfect and precise as Dr. Clarke insisted when I was in high school, people think you're wise, and most of the time, when people approached me, it was because they needed my advice. Fortunately, the primitive minds of ancient Rome—even its aristocratic ruling class—were easy for a twenty-first-century intellect to impress. I had the benefit of almost two millennia of scientists, mathematicians, and philosophers to call upon, though more often than not, my pearls of wisdom were more pop culture references.

"*Longa vita et bene,*" I said as I made up some excuse, or else the fuller would talk my ear off all day with all the latest gossip, holding up my hand in a cryptic V symbol nobody recognized. When asked, I told people that it was a blessing from Vulcan.

It means "live long and prosper."

"Watch out for the sand, Io," Marcus warned me one day as we traversed the uneven cobblestone streets. "It can be quite slippery after a rainfall."

"Thank you, Marcus," I replied, grateful for his constant guidance. "I'll keep that in mind."

As we walked side by side, I couldn't help but feel a deepening connection between us. Marcus was more than just my mentor—he was my friend, and perhaps something more. I longed to share my true origin with him, but fear held me back. Would he still accept me if he knew that I was not of this world?

"Marcus," I began hesitantly, "do you ever wonder about the future?"

"Sometimes." His gaze met mine, and I could see the curiosity in his eyes. "Why do you ask?"

"Because…" I paused, unsure how to phrase my thoughts. "I often think of what life will be like for the generations to come. Will they remember us? Will they learn from our mistakes?"

"Perhaps." He smiled gently. "But all we can do is live our lives the best we can and hope that those who follow will do the same."

"Indeed," I replied, taking comfort in his words. For now, at least, I would continue to embrace my new life and the man who had made it possible. And maybe, one day, I would find the courage to tell him the truth.

* * *

My knowledge of Latin continued to serve me well in this strange old world. The locals marveled at my fluency, and I even became adept in the vulgar slang that peppered daily conversation. As a result, I found myself able to connect with people from all walks of life—from the merchants hawking their wares in the bustling forum to the laborers who toiled under the hot Mediterranean sun.

"*Salve*, Iosephus!" called out Decimus, a cheerful baker whose shop wafted the tantalizing scent of freshly baked bread throughout the street. "You must try my latest creation—it is stuffed with olives and cheese!"

"*Gratias tibi ago, Decimus*," I replied, accepting the warm loaf with a nod of appreciation. "I'm happy to see you're incorporating some unusual ingredients into your baking."

"Ah, but it is thanks to you that I have been inspired to experiment!" he exclaimed, his eyes lighting up with pride. "Your tales of far-off lands and exotic flavors have sparked my imagination. How fortunate we are to have you here in Pompeii!"

"*Longa vita et bene*, Decimus," I said with a smile, raising my hand in the familiar Vulcan salute. He chuckled, his round face creasing into a grin as he attempted to mimic the gesture.

"Ah, Io, always full of surprises! *Vale!*" he called out as I continued on my way.

One day, while conversing with a group of friends in the local tavern, I accidentally let slip an English phrase.

"*Carpe diem!* Seize the day!" I declared, raising my cup in a toast. Then, without thinking, I added, "You only live once, after all."

"*Quid dicis, Io?*" asked Gaius, the owner of the tavern, looking puzzled. "What language was that?"

"Um... Celtic," I lied, feeling a flush rise to my cheeks. "The language of my homeland."

"Ah, Celtic! Fascinating," remarked Lucius, a well-traveled trader who had joined our gathering. "I've heard it spoken in the far north, but never here in Pompeii."

"Indeed," I replied, hoping my embarrassment was not too evident. "I do enjoy learning new languages—it's a window into other cultures. That's why I learned your Latin."

"And learned it well," Decimus noted. "You sound like a senator."

My friends nodded in agreement, and we continued our conversation late into the night, swapping stories and sharing laughter.

As the months passed, I delved deeper into the rich tapestry of Pompeian life, using my linguistic skills and historical knowledge to navigate this ancient world. And though I was still haunted by the weight of my secret, I found solace in the connections I forged with the people around me. Their resilience, their joy, and their unwavering acceptance of me as one of their own offered a sense of belonging I had never thought possible.

But despite these comforts, I knew that the sands of time were slipping away, and with each passing day, the shadow of Vesuvius loomed ever larger.

* * *

The sun was setting, casting a warm orange glow over the city as Marcus and I walked along the cobbled streets of Pompeii, our fingers entwined. Over time, our friendship had blossomed into something deeper, something neither of us had expected but both welcomed with open hearts.

As we continued walking, I couldn't help but think about how much Marcus had helped me navigate this world. He had taught me the intricacies of Roman etiquette and customs, patiently explaining everything from the proper way to wear a toga to the significance of various religious rituals.

"Remember that time you tried to explain the concept of 'rock-paper-scissors' to the children playing in the forum?" Marcus asked, grinning at the memory.

"Ah yes, a game from my homeland," I said, chuckling. "They were so confused when I kept losing to their 'rock' with my 'scissors.' Little did they know it was all part of my grand strategy."

"Your cunning knows no bounds, Io," Marcus laughed, nudging me playfully.

"Speaking of which," I said, suddenly serious. "I've been meaning to ask you...would you like to join me for a picnic tomorrow atop Mount Vesuvius? The view is said to be spectacular, especially during the sunset."

"Of course, I would love to," he replied without hesitation. "It's a date."

The next day, as we climbed the steep path leading up to the summit of Vesuvius, I couldn't shake the feeling of dread that settled in my chest. My breaths came out in short gasps, and it wasn't just from the exertion. Marcus, ever observant, furrowed his brow in concern.

"Are you alright, Io?" he asked, pausing to catch his breath. "You seem...nervous."

"Ah, it's nothing," I lied, attempting a reassuring smile. "I'm just not used to climbing mountains, that's all."

"Very well," he said, though the worry remained etched upon his face.

As we reached the summit and spread out our picnic blanket, the breathtaking view of Pompeii stretched out below us, its terracotta rooftops bathed in the golden light of the setting sun. But even this magnificent sight could not dispel my unease.

"Marcus, there's something I should tell you," I began hesitantly, my heart pounding in my chest.

"Is everything alright?" he asked, concern creasing his handsome features.

"Truthfully, I..." I trailed off, unable to find the words. How could I explain to him who I really was, where I truly came from, and the impending doom that awaited these people I had come to love?

"Is it the mountain?" he asked softly, noticing the fear in my eyes. "Are you afraid?"

"Perhaps a little," I admitted, swallowing hard. "But it's more than that. There's something I need to tell you, but I don't know how."

"Whatever it is, Io," Marcus said, taking my hand in his, "know that I am here for you, and I will stand by your side, no matter what."

"Thank you," I whispered, my eyes brimming with unshed

tears. "I just hope that when the time comes, I'll have the courage to share my truth with you."

As the sun dipped below the horizon, bathing the city in a warm embrace, I held Marcus close, knowing that whatever lay ahead, our love would endure. And perhaps, through this love, I might find the strength to face the future and protect those I cared about most, even if it meant defying the very fabric of history itself.

* * *

The warm sun shone down on the bustling streets of Pompeii, casting long shadows as I walked alongside Marcus. Our laughter mingled with the chatter of merchants and customers haggling over prices at the market stalls. As we strolled through the heart of the city, I couldn't help but marvel at my new life, so different from anything I had ever imagined.

"Ah, Io! There you are!" a familiar voice called out, breaking me from my reverie.

"*Salve*, Gaius!" I greeted the procurator. He was a stout man, with a quick wit and an infectious laugh. "Perfect timing," Gaius boomed, slapping me on the back. "We're just about to head to the tavern for a drink. Care to join us?"

"Sounds delightful," Marcus chimed in, his eyes twinkling.

As we made our way to the tavern, I noticed how easily I had come to fit into this world. My Latin, precise and perfect, allowed me to communicate with the locals effortlessly. Even the most skeptical citizens came to respect me, often seeking my counsel on various matters. It was astonishing how much knowledge I had retained from my studies, which now proved invaluable in navigating this ancient society.

"Tell us again, Io, what was that you said about the needs of the many?" Antonius asked as we settled around a table, flagons of wine in hand.

"Ah, yes," I said, grinning. "The needs of the many outweigh the needs of the few. A wise man from my homeland taught me that. His logic was impeccable." Unable to resist, I added. "He was as devoted worshipper of Vulcan as there ever was."

"Indeed," Petrus agreed, nodding solemnly. "Did he also teach you that phrase you use as a farewell? The one with the peculiar hand gesture?"

"*Longa vita et bene,*" I demonstrated, spreading my fingers to form a V. I held up my hand and smiled. "It's an ancient blessing from Vulcan."

"Excuse me, Iosephus Andrius?" a stranger approached, addressing me by my Romanized name. He was an older man, stooped with age but still possessing a keen intelligence in his eyes. "I am Nuntius, a friend of Salvius, and I bring news from the empire."

"*Salve*, Nuntius," I greeted him, shaking his outstretched hand. "We met my first night here. *Grata!* Please, join us."

As we spent the afternoon discussing politics, philosophy, and our shared love for Pompeii, I marveled at how far I had come. In just a few short months, I had become an informed and involved citizen of this ancient city. And despite the occasional slip into English—which my friends mistook for Celtic—I felt a sense of belonging I had never experienced before.

"Here's to Io," Nintius declared, raising his cup high. "A true citizen of Pompeii!"

"Cheers!" came the chorus of voices around the table, and I couldn't help but smile, feeling both grateful and humbled by their acceptance.

"May the gods continue to bless our beloved city," I said softly, sipping my wine, allowing the warmth of friendship and love to envelop me like a comforting embrace.

* * *

The sun had just begun to set, casting long shadows across the stone pavements of Pompeii. I stood in the courtyard of my new home, watching as Petrus and Tiberius played a friendly game of dice. Their laughter echoed through the air, mingling with the soft sounds of Antonius strumming his *cithara*.

"Ah, Io, there you are!" Flavius called out, emerging from the kitchen with a platter of steaming stuffed dormice. "Come, try one! They're fresh and delicious."

"Thank you, Flavius," I said, taking one hesitantly, still not fully accustomed to this Roman delicacy. As I bit into the tender meat, I couldn't help but think of how far I'd come. Just three months ago, I was living in my own time, struggling to find meaning in my life. Now, here I was—Iosephus Andrius—a respected citizen of ancient Pompeii.

"Is everything alright, Io?" Marcus asked, his brow furrowed with concern as he noticed my distant expression.

"Of course," I replied, forcing a smile. "I was just thinking about how lucky I am to have found such wonderful friends here."

"Indeed, we are all fortunate to have each other," Marcus agreed, placing a reassuring hand on my shoulder.

But as much as I tried to appreciate my newfound life, a nagging feeling gnawed at me. I was an impostor, a man out of time masquerading as someone I wasn't. These people—my friends—trusted and respected me, and yet they knew nothing of my true nature.

"Would they still accept me if they knew the truth?" I wondered silently, the weight of my dishonesty pressing down on me.

My thoughts took an even darker turn when I considered what awaited these unsuspecting souls. In less than a year, Vesuvius would erupt, burying Pompeii and everyone in it beneath a torrent of ash and pumice. My friends—my new family—were all doomed to die.

"Can I change history?" I questioned myself. "Should I even try?" The moral implications of such a decision terrified me. Was it right for me to interfere with the natural course of time? What if my actions caused even greater suffering?

"Are you sure you're alright, Io?" Marcus asked again, his eyes searching mine for any hint of distress. "You seem...troubled."

"Nothing's wrong," I lied, trying to push my troubling thoughts aside. "Just enjoying this beautiful evening."

"Good," he said, giving me a warm smile. "Remember, you can

always talk to me about anything."

"Thank you, Marcus," I whispered, touched by his unwavering support. But despite his kind words, I couldn't bring myself to share my secret burden with him.

As the sun dipped below the horizon, bathing Pompeii in twilight, I joined my friends as they gathered around a flickering fire. Our voices filled the night with laughter and song, a fleeting moment of joy amidst the mounting storm of my conscience.

"May the gods watch over us all," I prayed silently, knowing that only time would reveal if I had the courage to act on my convictions—or if I would let history take its tragic course.

* * *

Over the next few weeks, my bond with Marcus grew stronger than I could have ever imagined. He was my confidant and my guide in this ancient world, helping me navigate the treacherous waters of Pompeian society. As much as I tried to hide my true nature from him, he seemed to understand me on a deeper level than anyone else in Pompeii.

"Come now, Io. You must try this," Marcus said, handing me a steaming bowl of barley porridge. We were sitting together in the bustling marketplace, enjoying breakfast amidst the chatter of merchants and townsfolk.

"Is it really that good?" I asked skeptically, taking a hesitant bite.

"Trust me," he assured me, his eyes twinkling with amusement.

To my surprise, the porridge was delicious—rich, creamy, and infused with the delicate flavors of saffron and honey. I couldn't help but laugh at the unexpected delight of the simple dish.

"See? I told you!" Marcus grinned, looking incredibly pleased with himself.

"Alright, alright," I conceded, wiping my mouth with a linen napkin. "You win this round."

As we continued our meal, I couldn't help but feel a surge of gratitude for Marcus's unwavering support. Despite my many fumbles and awkward moments, he never once judged me or made me feel like an outsider. It was as if he somehow sensed the burden of my secret, even though he didn't know what it was.

"Marcus," I ventured, hesitating for a moment before continuing. "I want you to know how much your friendship means to me. You've been there for me through everything, and I can't thank you enough."

"Of course, Io," he replied softly, his gaze warm and sincere. "That's what friends are for."

As much as I longed to share my true self with him, the risk was too great. I couldn't bear the thought of losing his trust—or worse, endangering him with the knowledge of my impossible secret.

One day, as we strolled through the bustling streets of Pompeii, I stumbled upon a familiar sight that stopped me in my tracks. There, near the entrance to a small temple, was a little old lady setting up the very shrine I had seen in the ruins back in my own time.

"May the gods watch over our beloved city and protect us from disaster," she murmured, her voice barely audible above the din of the crowd.

Suddenly, it felt as if the weight of my decision came crashing down upon me. If I chose to act—to somehow save these people from their fate—could I really be sure that I was doing the right thing? Even if I could change history, should I?

"Maybe the gods brought me here for a reason," I pondered, my gaze fixed on the aged woman tending to the shrine. As much as I longed to prevent the tragedy that loomed over Pompeii, I couldn't shake the feeling that perhaps some things were simply meant to be. "But what reason? I don't know!"

"Marcus," I whispered, my voice trembling with uncertainty. "What would you do if you knew something terrible was going to happen? Would you try to stop it, even if it meant changing the course of history?"

He looked thoughtful for a moment before answering. "I suppose it would depend on the situation," he admitted, his brow furrowing with concern. "But ultimately, I believe that we are all bound by a greater destiny—one that is beyond our control."

"Destiny," I echoed, the word resonating deep within me. As I stood there, watching the little old lady carefully arrange the offerings on the shrine, I knew what I had to do. No matter how much I cared for Marcus and the people of Pompeii, I couldn't interfere with the natural order of time.

"Thank you, Marcus," I murmured, the weight of my decision settling heavily upon my shoulders. "You always know just what to say."

"Anything for you, Io," he replied, his eyes filled with a warmth and understanding that almost made me believe he knew my secret after all.

* * *

As I stood on the rooftop of Villa Marcelli, I couldn't help but marvel at the beauty of this ancient place—a beauty that would soon be lost to the sands of time.

"Io," Marcus called from behind me, his voice filled with concern. "You've been up here for hours. Are you all right?"

I turned to face him, their genuine worry etched across his handsome features. "I've been thinking, Marcus," I confessed, my heart heavy with the burden of my impending decision. "About what we discussed earlier... about destiny."

"Ah," he nodded, stepping closer and resting a hand on my shoulder. "It's a difficult subject, I know. But remember, Io, we cannot control the fates. All we can do is live our lives to the fullest and trust in the gods' plan."

"Trusting in the gods' plan," I echoed, considering his words carefully. Though I had initially resolved not to interfere with the natural order of time, I couldn't shake the feeling that there must be some way for me to save the people I had grown to love. The friendships I had formed here were strong, and I knew that I could not stand idly by while disaster loomed. "But we hire augurs to predict the future."

"The augurs serve an important role," Marcus pointed out. "They tell us when to plant our crops, and when to harvest."

"We have people like that where I live. We call them meteorologists. All they know is how to read the signs—a red sky in the morning means it's going to rain. It's not magic."

"What are you talking about?"

"Marcus," I began hesitantly, my eyes darting to his for reassurance. "Your people don't realize it yet, but Vesuvius is a 'fire mountain' like Etna, only much more powerful. When it awakens it will unleash power the likes of which humans have never seen before, and it will annihilate the people of Pompeii and Herculaneum. I have seen this. I have walked through the ruins." I sighed. "What if there was a way to save at least some people? To warn them about what's coming without them thinking I'm mad.?"

He regarded me seriously, his brow furrowing as he pondered my question. After a moment, he replied, "If such a possibility existed, I believe it would be our duty to try. We may not be able to change the course of history entirely, but perhaps we can lessen the suffering."

"Exactly," I agreed, a newfound determination surging through me. "I can't just do nothing. I have to try to save as many people as possible."

"Then let us begin," Marcus said resolutely, his eyes shining with conviction. "Together, we will find a way."

Over the next several days, we began to devise a plan. We would subtly spread rumors of impending doom—whispers of strange omens and signs from the gods—in the hopes that it would be enough to convince some of the citizens to flee before it was too late.

"Did you hear about the strange smell near the mountain?" I asked Marcus one evening, feigning concern as we dined together at the local tavern. "Some say it's a sign that the gods are displeased."

"It is the smell of brimstone," Marcus said with a teasing smile. "The flatulence of the gods."

I laughed at the thought of God farting.

"I believe it is an omen," I said with a serious tone. "I have seen these signs before, and they do not bode well."

Marcus stared at me in awe. "And you have seen this?"

What the hell. "Yes, Marcus, I have. I must take you into my confidence." I made sure we were alone and lowered my voice. "I have had a vision, Marcus. I've seen the destruction of Pompeii."

Marcus' face blanched. "Are you sure?"

"There is no mistake. I have seen the city in ruins. Bodies buried alive, their death throes frozen in time."

Marcus gasped. "When?"

The answer was easy. Vesuvius erupted in October 79, four months after the death of Emperor Vespasian. But I couldn't just tell Marcus that without having to answer some very hard questions. "Soon. But there will be signs."

"What signs?"

"First the Emperor will fall," I answered. "Four moons later Pompeii will be destroyed."

"We must tell someone!"

"It is too soon. I have no proof. But Vespasian will die—next summer, I think. Four months later..." I didn't need to finish that sentence. "Maybe it was just a bad dream, but I remember it was the month of Juno.

"Chronos." Marcus nodded. "We must talk to Chronos."

"Chronos?"

"Chronos the Soothsayer. He is the town augur. Surely, he will know what to do."

CHAPTER VII

As we entered the dimly lit abode of Chronos the Soothsayer, I couldn't help but shudder involuntarily. The air was thick with incense and mystery, sending a chill down my spine. Mystic artifacts cluttered the room, casting eerie shadows on the walls. In the center of the room stood a large crystal ball, its surface swirling with an ethereal mist.

Chronos himself was an unsettling sight. A tall, thin man, his gaunt frame draped in tattered robes, he looked like a specter from another world. His eyes were sunken deep into his skull, and when they met mine, it felt as if he were staring straight through me. He regarded both Marcus and me with cold disinterest, his boney fingers tapping impatiently on the table beside his crystal ball.

"*Salve,*" I began, trying to introduce myself. "My name is—"

"Save your breath, Iosephus Andrius," Chronos interrupted, his voice high-pitched and cackling. "I already know who you are, Celt."

I exchanged a puzzled look with Marcus before turning back to the soothsayer. "But how? We've never met before."

"Ah, but I know many things about you," Chronos replied, leaning forward and narrowing his eyes. "Things that would make a lesser man tremble in fear." Obviously, he didn't know because if he knew who I really was, then he would understand how I knew the future. Still, his words unnerved me. What could he possibly know?

"Such as?" I challenged, trying to suppress the unease growing in my chest. "Where am I from?"

"Alexandria. You have said so yourself."

"Ah, but which Alexandria? There are many cities that bear that name. Which one do I call home?"

Chronos stared at me coldly. "I care not."

"I come from the Land of Minnesota," I responded, "from the Empire of America."

"I know of no land of Minnesota, nor any Empire of America."

"Well, now," I smirked, "I guess you're not as all-seeing as you'd have us believe, then."

I would later learn that it was the only time anybody had ever seen Chronos struck speechless. He waved dismissively. "Your arrival in Pompeii was no accident, man from Minnesota," he whispered, a sinister grin spreading across his face. "And neither will be your departure."

I glanced at Marcus, who seemed to be just as confused as I was. This was not going as planned. The tension in the room was palpable, and I could feel Chronos's mistrust growing stronger by the second.

"Listen," I said, trying to steer the conversation in a different direction, "we came here seeking your guidance. There is something I need to tell you, something of great importance."

"He must be heard!" Marcus pleaded. "Lives are at stake!"

"Speak then," Chronos snapped, his eyes fixed on me with an intensity that made my skin crawl.

I hesitated for a moment, choosing my words carefully before launching into what I hoped would be a convincing story. The fate of Pompeii rested on my ability to persuade this man, and I couldn't afford to let him see how uncertain I truly felt.

"Very well," I said finally, taking a deep breath. "But remember—you asked for it."

I took a deep breath, feeling the weight of the prophecy on my shoulders. "I have seen a vision, Chronos," I began, my voice steady and clear. "A vision of doom and destruction that will befall Pompeii and Herculaneum."

"Go on," Chronos prompted, his eyes narrowing suspiciously.

"Vespasian, our great emperor, shall soon pass from this world, and may the gods grant him eternal peace. Four moons later, the mighty god Vulcan will awaken in a fury. His wrath will rain down upon Pompeii, smiting it from the face of the earth."

"Ha!" Chronos barked out a laugh, his hyena-like cackle echoing through the dimly lit room. "You think you can predict the future, Minnesota? Leave such matters to those who are truly gifted with foresight."

"Chronos," Marcus interjected, his voice calm but firm, "Io is sincere in his beliefs. Is it not worth considering that his vision may hold some truth?"

"I speak the truth!" I insisted. "The vision was clear! Thousands of voices cried out in terror and were suddenly silenced!"

"Silence!" Chronos snapped, glaring at Marcus. "You drank too much wine," he said dismissively, "and had a bad dream. This is of no concern to me."

"Chronos, if what I say is true—" I tried to appeal to him, but he cut me off.

"Enough!" he snarled, his anger bubbling up like lava from Vesuvius' depths. "I am the town augur, and it is my duty to interpret the signs given to us by the gods. You are but an intruder, meddling in affairs far beyond your comprehension."

"Please, just consider the possibility—" Chronos waved his arm toward the door to dismiss us, and I saw for the first time the amulet hanging around his neck. The circular amulet with a seven-pointed star and the green stone at the center. The same charm that brought me here. "You *know!*" I said in shock, backing away. "You *know* about the volcano! You *know* and you aren't telling them!"

"Get out!" Chronos roared, his skeletal frame trembling with rage. "Leave my presence and never return! Your foolish attempts at divination insult the gods, and I will no longer suffer your presence!"

I stared at him in disbelief, my heart pounding in my chest. How could he dismiss my warning so easily? The lives of thousands hung in the balance, but his pride blinded him to the truth.

"Come on, Io," Marcus said softly, placing a hand on my shoulder. "We should go."

As we left Chronos's dimly lit chamber, I couldn't help but feel a sense of dread creeping over me. If even the town augur refused to heed my warning, what hope did Pompeii have?

"Marcus," I whispered as we stepped into the sunlight, "what if no one believes me? What if I can't save them?"

"Have faith, Io," Marcus replied, squeezing my shoulder reassuringly. "The truth has a way of making itself known. And perhaps others will be more receptive to your message than Chronos was."

I nodded, trying to hold onto hope. But as we walked away from Chronos' home, I couldn't shake the feeling that time was running out for Pompeii—and that it might already be too late to change its fate. When I found that amulet in the future, it was buried in ash, so at least I had the small satisfaction of knowing that his fate was already sealed.

* * *

"Io, is it true?" Marcus asked nervously after we left, my disappointment palpable as we left Chronos's home. "Will Pompeii be destroyed?"

"Vespasian will die first," I murmured. "Pompeii will fall four months later. The vision is clear."

"You speak in riddles, Io," Marcus said with a concerned expression, but before I could respond, a man stepped into our path.

"I have to. I don't think anyone can handle the tru—"

"Excuse me," a stranger said, holding up a hand to stop us. "Io, is that you?" I recognized him from the tavern. He wrote for the *Actus Diurna*… he was the media! "I couldn't help but overhear your conversation." The stranger was slender and wore the simple garb of a scribe. His eyes held a curious gleam as he studied us intently.

"Yes, you're the scribe, right?" I asked warily, .

"Yes, I am," he beamed proudly. "I transcribe the *Actus Diurna* for our fair city." He paused, studying my face for a moment. "And it sounds like you have quite a story to tell. Tell me more about this prophecy, if you would."

"Prophecy?" I hesitated, exchanging a glance with Marcus. Could I trust this man with such knowledge?

"Indeed," Lucius urged. "If what you say is true, the people of Pompeii must know."

I took a deep breath, weighing the risks. "Very well," I conceded. "As I told Chronos, I have seen the destruction of Pompeii. The first sign will be when Vespasian dies. Four moons later, Vulcan shall arise from Mount Vesuvius and smite Pompeii from the face of the earth."

"Vespasian is going to die?" Lucius pondered aloud, his eyes widening in surprise. "How can you know such things?"

"Let's just say I have... visions," I replied cryptically, unwilling to reveal my time-traveling secret. "They've never been wrong."

"Remarkable," Lucius murmured, his excitement barely contained. "This is a story that must be shared with the people of Pompeii."

"Are you sure?" Marcus interjected, his voice laced with concern. "Chronos, the town augur, dismissed Io's prophecy as nonsense."

"Chronos has been wrong before," Lucius said dismissively. "The people deserve to know the truth, and I will ensure they hear it."

With that, Lucius hurried away, leaving Marcus and me to contemplate the consequences of our actions. As we walked through the busy streets of Pompeii, the sun casting long shadows over the bustling market, I couldn't help but wonder if sharing my prophecy would do more harm than good. Only time would tell if the citizens of Pompeii would heed the warning—or if their fate was already set in stone.

By the gods, I thought, what have I done?

* * *

The sun had dipped below the horizon as I entered Domus Marcelli, a warm and inviting home filled with the intoxicating scents of incense and exotic spices. The flickering light from oil lamps danced across the walls, casting the residence in a golden glow. Salvius welcomed me with open arms, while Quintus was sitting in a corner sketching with charcoal.

"Quintus has been a bit troubled lately," Salvus explained quietly, concern etched on his face. "His ex-lover, Felix, has joined a cult called the Followers. It's all he can think about."

I nodded sympathetically, recalling my own past heartaches. As we stood there, Quintus approached us, his dark eyes holding a storm of emotions behind them. He seemed hesitant but determined to speak with me.

"Father tells me you're a man of knowledge, Io," he began, his voice soft but firm. "Perhaps you could help me better understand what Felix is going through."

I took a deep breath, preparing myself for the conversation ahead. "I'll do my best, Quintus," I replied gently, guiding him towards a quiet corner of the room.

"Have you ever heard of this cult, the Followers?" he asked, his brow furrowed with worry.

"Unfortunately, I have," I admitted, my heart aching for the young man before me. "Their beliefs can be quite dangerous to themselves and others. As I understand, their very existence has been prohibited by Caesar, and wisely so."

Quintus sighed, his shoulders slumping in defeat. "Felix was never one for religion, and now... it's like he's become someone else entirely."

As we spoke, I couldn't help but notice the various works of art adorning the walls of Domus Marcelli. Quintus seemed to follow my gaze, a small, proud smile playing at his lips.

"Are you the artist behind these beautiful pieces, Quintus?" I inquired, genuinely impressed by the skill and emotion displayed in each painting.

He nodded, blushing slightly. "Yes, art has always been a way for me to express myself, to make sense of the world around me. Father says I am quite good."

"Your talent is undeniable," I praised him, my eyes lingering on a particular piece that felt eerily familiar. It was a stunning depiction of Mount Vesuvius, bathed in an ethereal light that seemed to emanate from within the canvas itself.

"Wait a moment," I murmured, my heart pounding in my chest as I stared at the painting. "I've seen this before... back in—."

"When did you see it before?" Quintus asked

"When I first got here," I said quickly, realizing my slip-up. "What I meant to say was, your work reminds me of something I once saw in a dream. A powerful image that has stayed with me ever since. It's Marcus, right?"

"Yes, it does." Quintus blushed. "Please don't tell him about it..."

"He hasn't seen this?" I looked at the painting with an approving nod. "He didn't pose for it?"

Quintus shook his head. "I did it from memory. Marcus is a beautiful man, is he not?" He smiled at me. "I've seen the way you look at each other. It brings me joy to see it." His smile frowned. "I remember when Felix looked at me that way."

"Your art is beautiful, Quintus. You do Marcus justice. I think he would be flattered, but it's totally up to you if you don't want to show him. Your secret is safe with me."

"Thank you, Io," Quintus replied, his smile genuine and warm. "That means more to me than you could possibly know."

As he spoke, I couldn't help but feel a connection forming between us, a bond forged through shared experiences and understanding. Though our lives were separated by millennia, we were both men navigating the complexities of love, loss, and self-discovery in a world that often seemed beyond our control.

And as the night wore on, the weight of my prophecy heavy on my mind, I knew that whatever challenges lay ahead, Quintus and I would face them together. For in the uncertain sands of time, our connections to others anchored us, grounding us in the present even as the future loomed large and unknown.

"Quintus," I said, as we stood together in his studio, the scent of oil paints and linseed filling the air. "There's something I need to talk to you about."

"Of course, Io." Quintus set aside his brush and turned to face me. His eyes were expectant, yet wary, as if he sensed the gravity of what I was about to say.

"It's about Felix," I began cautiously. "I know how much you still care for him, and I understand how difficult it must be to see him caught up in the Followers."

Quintus frowned but nodded for me to continue. "Yes, it has been hard, but what can I do?"

"From my own experiences," I said, recalling the painful dissolution of my relationship with Mark, "sometimes all you can do is offer support and understanding. But in this case, there may be more at stake. This cult, the Followers, could pose a danger not only to Felix but to others as well."

"What kind of danger?" Quintus's voice was barely a whisper.

"I've seen groups like this back in… well, where I come from," I said, almost revealing my true origin again. "They can become fanatical, extreme, even violent. They prey on people who are vulnerable, like Felix. He may not realize the risks he's taking by becoming involved with them."

"By Jupiter," Quintus murmured, anguish clouding his eyes. "What should I do, Io?"

"First, don't give up on him," I advised. "Remind him of who he was before the cult—the man you loved. Show him that you still care and that there's a life waiting for him outside the grips of the Followers."

"Would that be enough?" Quintus asked doubtfully.

"Perhaps not," I admitted. "But it's a start. You can also inform the local authorities if you feel the cult is becoming a threat. They may be able to intervene and protect both Felix and others who have been ensnared."

"Thank you, Io," Quintus said earnestly. "I appreciate your advice more than you know."

"Of course, my friend," I replied warmly.

Over the days that followed, Quintus and I spent hours together, discussing art, politics, and life in Pompeii. As we strolled through the bustling streets, he would point out the intricate details of the city—the frescoes on the walls of shops, the worn inscriptions on the tombs along the Via delle Tombe, and even the vibrant colors of the fish in the market, caught fresh from the Bay of Naples. Our conversations were filled with laughter and light-hearted banter, but beneath it all was an undercurrent of trust and understanding.

"Did you know," Quintus mused one day as we enjoyed cups of sweetened wine at a *popina*, "that some people believe the murals in our bathhouses possess magical properties? They think that if you touch them in just the right way, they can bring luck or even cure ailments."

"Really?" I asked, intrigued by this piece of obscure history.

"Indeed," Quintus replied with a grin. "Though personally, I've never had any success with them."

"Perhaps you're not touching them correctly," I teased, raising an eyebrow playfully.

"Or perhaps the magic is reserved for those like you, Io, who seem to possess a rare wisdom beyond their years," he countered, his eyes twinkling with mirth.

As our friendship deepened, I felt a profound sense of belonging that I hadn't experienced since arriving in Pompeii. In Quintus, I had found someone who saw me not as a stranger or an oddity, but as a fellow traveler on life's winding path. And though the shadow of my prophecy loomed ever closer, I took solace in the knowledge that I had made a true and lasting connection that would endure, even as the sands of time continued to shift beneath our feet.

* * *

I walked through the bustling streets of Pompeii, taking in the sights and sounds that surrounded me. The smell of freshly baked bread wafted through the air as I passed by a bakery, its owner calling out to potential customers. As I continued along, I spotted a group of people huddled around a man with a scroll in his hand. Curiosity piqued, I moved closer to see what was happening.

"Lucius, the scribe from the *Actus Diurna!*" Quintus whispered beside me, having caught up with my strides. "He's reading aloud the news he's transcribed."

"Listen, dear citizens," Lucius began, drawing the crowd's attention. "A prophecy has been told—one that could change the fate of our beloved city. A man named Io claims to have seen the destruction of Pompeii. He warns us that the first sign will be when Emperor Vespasian dies, and just four moons later, Vulcan will arise and smite our city from the face of the earth!"

The crowd murmured uneasily, glancing at one another with worried expressions. I felt a cold knot form in my stomach, realizing that my prophecy had now spread far beyond the walls of Chronos' dimly lit lair. My words were no longer just between Marcus, Quintus, and myself—they were now etched into the minds of every person who heard Lucius' report. The weight of responsibility for this knowledge settled heavily upon my shoulders.

"Prophecies are nothing new," a woman scoffed, breaking through the tense silence. "How can we trust this stranger?"

"Indeed!" another man chimed in. "What does this Io know of our city? Of our gods? How dare he foretell our doom?"

"Perhaps," said an elderly gent, stroking his beard thoughtfully, "this Io speaks the truth, and we should heed his warning."

"Preposterous!" a younger man countered. "I don't believe in such nonsense. It's just fear-mongering by an outsider!"

The crowd began to disperse, still arguing as they went their separate ways. I could feel the eyes of those who remained, sizing me up and whispering amongst themselves. It was clear that some considered me a threat—a harbinger of doom—while others saw me as a madman or a charlatan.

"Come," Quintus urged, pulling me away from the crowd. "We best be on our way before you become the center of attention." He dragged me insistently around a corner.

As we made our way through the city, I couldn't shake the feeling of unease that had settled upon me. What if my prophecy did more harm than good? What if its very utterance brought about the destruction I sought to prevent?

"Quintus," I whispered, "perhaps it was a mistake to share my vision with Chronos. The people are scared, and I don't know how to reassure them."

"Prophecies have a way of shaking things up," he replied gently. "But sometimes, change is necessary."

"Even when it threatens everything we hold dear?"

"Especially then," he said solemnly. "For it is only through adversity that true strength is revealed."

Unbeknownst to us, Chronos had been lurking nearby, his cold gaze fixed on me with undisguised contempt. As he watched the scene unfold, his anger at my growing influence within Pompeii reached a boiling point.

"Mark my words, Io," he hissed under his breath. "You may have the ear of the people for now, but I will expose you for the fraud you are. And when I do, your precious prophecy will be nothing more than ashes on the wind."

And with that dark promise, Chronos retreated into the shadows, nursing his wounded pride and plotting his revenge.

* * *

The Pompeian sun beat down mercilessly on the Forum, casting long shadows across the bustling marketplace. Sweat trickled down my neck as I weaved through the throngs of merchants and citizens, the cacophony of voices blending with the scent of fresh bread and ripe fruit. Quintus walked beside me, his expression troubled. "Look," he said, pointing towards a group gathered around a messenger. "Lucius's news has certainly spread."

I took a deep breath, steeling myself for the confrontation I knew was coming. As if sensing my thoughts, Chronos emerged from the crowd, his gaunt face twisted in a sneer. He strode towards me, his skeletal frame making him appear like some apparition of death.

"Ah, the soothsayer of doom," he cackled, drawing the attention of passersby. "It seems you have made quite the impression upon our simple-minded townsfolk."

"Chronos," I replied, my voice steady despite my heart pounding. "My intentions are pure. I only wish to warn the people—"

"Ha!" he scoffed, his eyes narrowing with malice. "And who are you to make such claims? An outsider who stumbles into our city with wild tales of destruction?"

"Is it not your duty as an augur to consider all possibilities?" I retorted, feeling the heat rise in my cheeks. "Or are your abilities limited to reading the birds' flights and the sacrificial animals' entrails?"

"Watch your tongue, boy," Chronos snarled, his boney fingers clenching into fists. "Do not presume to question my knowledge or my dedication to this city."

"Then why do you dismiss my prophecy out of hand?" I asked, meeting his cold gaze without flinching. "Are you afraid that my words might prove true, and your own powers inadequate?"

"Enough!" Chronos roared, his voice carrying across the Forum. "You are nothing more than a charlatan, spreading chaos and panic among our people. I will expose you for the fraud you are!"

"Are you so certain of your own infallibility?" I shot back, stepping closer to him. "Or is it merely your pride that blinds you to the truth?"

"Silence!" he bellowed, raising his hand as if to strike me.

"Stop this at once!" a deep voice boomed, cutting through the tense atmosphere. The *vigiles urbani*, clad in their distinctive red tunics and bronze helmets, marched towards us, stern expressions etched on their faces.

"Disperse, all of you," one of the officers commanded as he stepped between Chronos and me. "This is not the place for such altercations."

"Very well," Chronos spat, fixing me with a venomous glare before turning away. "But mark my words, Io: this is far from over."

* * *

"Chronos has never been one to back down from a challenge," Marcus said, glancing over his shoulder as if expecting the soothsayer to materialize behind us. "But you handled yourself well."

"Thank you," I mumbled, my thoughts turning inward. I knew

I had to tread carefully around Chronos; he was a powerful figure in Pompeii, and making an enemy of him could have disastrous consequences. But I also couldn't ignore the heavy weight of responsibility that rested on my shoulders. I had seen the destruction of Pompeii, even if it was through the eyes of a man from another time. And I would do everything in my power to save these people—even if it meant going toe-to-toe with one of the most feared men in the city.

"Whatcha thinking?" Marcus asked, breaking into my reverie.

"About the prophecy," I admitted. "I can't help but wonder if anyone will actually believe me—or if they'll dismiss me as a madman."

"Only time will tell," Marcus said, his tone somber. "But I know one thing for certain: you've got guts, Io. And that counts for something."

"Thanks, Marcus," I murmured, touched by his show of support.

"Besides," he continued, a mischievous glint entering his eyes, "if Chronos can't handle a little competition, maybe it's time for him to step down as Pompeii's resident soothsayer."

"Let's not get ahead of ourselves," I warned him, chuckling softly. "I'm no seer—just a man who happened to glimpse the future."

"Still, there's something to be said for challenging the status quo," Marcus insisted. "And if your prophecy comes true, that'll certainly shake things up around here."

"Indeed," I agreed, my thoughts turning once more to the fiery destruction that awaited this city and its inhabitants. I glanced around at the people going about their daily routines, unaware of the danger lurking beneath their feet. And despite the uncertainty that clouded my vision, I knew one thing beyond all doubt: I would do everything in my power to save them—or die trying.

CHAPTER VIII

The abandoned Etruscan temple loomed on the outskirts of town, a ghostly relic that seemed to defy time itself. Its once-grand walls now crumbled under the weight of history, surrendering to the relentless embrace of ivy and vines. The eerie silence that permeated the air only served to amplify the whispers of the past, as if the spirits of those long gone still lingered within its depths.

Within the shadowed confines of the temple, the flickering candlelight revealed an assembly of hushed figures, their features obscured by the dancing shadows. At the center of it all stood Ovidius Aurius, the enigmatic leader of the outlaw cult, the Followers. His tall, imposing figure commanded attention, even amongst the crumbling ruins. The piercing gaze that emanated from his eyes seemed to peer into the very souls of those who stood before him, while his voice echoed through the stone chamber with an authority that demanded obedience.

"Brothers and sisters," he began, his words resonating like thunder in the still air, "we gather here tonight in defiance of those who would seek to silence our faith. We are the chosen few, the true believers who walk the path of the One."

The gathered Followers nodded in agreement, their faces a mixture of reverence and fear. They knew that their meetings were a dangerous game; they risked their lives for what they believed in, and that made them all the more devoted to their cause. In the eyes of Rome, they were outcasts, criminals. But to one another, they were family, bound by the shared belief in something greater than themselves.

Standing to the right of Ovidius, his second in command, Caius, exuded an intimidating presence. His muscular build and scarred face were a testament to the battles he had fought, both for his faith and against those who dared to challenge it. The aggressive demeanor that seemed to emanate from him was almost palpable, like a coiled viper ready to strike at the slightest provocation.

"Listen well, brothers and sisters," Ovidius continued, "for I shall speak of the One and the teachings brought to us by Paulus, our prophet." He turned to Caius, giving him a nod of approval. Caius stepped forward, his voice deep and unwavering.

"Paulus was chosen by the One to reveal His truth to the world," he began. "Through divine revelation, Paulus came to understand the true nature of the One's love and the path we must follow to achieve salvation."

"Romans have their gods, but they are false idols," Ovidius interjected, his voice filled with scorn. "Their debauchery and corruption know no bounds, but we, the Followers, have been shown the way by the One through Paulus. We reject the sinful ways of Rome and embrace the purity of the One's teachings."

"Indeed," Caius said, his eyes scanning the gathered Followers. "We believe in the sanctity of the family unit, as ordained by the One. We reject the hedonistic practices and lustful desires that run rampant in this empire. It is only by adhering to the tenets laid out by Paulus that we can find true fulfillment and purpose."

As Caius spoke, the faces of the Followers reflected their conviction and devotion to the cause. They hung on every word, determined to uphold the values espoused by their faith leader, Paulus. In a world where they felt lost and marginalized, the teachings of the One offered solace and meaning.

Under the law, these practices were punishable by death.

"Let us not forget the sacrifices made by our brothers and sisters who have come before us," Ovidius said solemnly. "Their blood has been spilled for our cause, and we must honor their memory by remaining steadfast in our faith."

"Under the guidance of Ovidius and the wisdom of Paulus, we shall continue to fight for our beliefs and protect the sanctity of the One's teachings," Caius declared. "We stand united, a beacon of hope in this dark and corrupted world."

"Indeed, we are the chosen ones," Ovidius affirmed, his voice resolute, "and we shall not waver." The Followers responded with fervent determination, their voices echoing through the ancient temple walls.

As the ceremony continued, it was clear that the Followers were more than just a group of outcasts seeking refuge from a society that shunned them; they were a force to be reckoned with, bound together by their unshakable faith in the One and the teachings of Paulus. And as long as they had each other, they would face whatever trials and tribulations lay ahead, unwavering in their devotion and commitment to their cause.

Felix Caerellius, the newest recruit of the Followers, stood near the crumbling walls of the abandoned Etruscan temple. His eyes darted nervously around the room, taking in the eerie silence and overgrown vines that seemed to grasp at his fears. He was a handsome young man with dark, wavy hair and deep-set green eyes that held a mixture of pain and curiosity. Despite his initial reluctance to join the cult, there was something about the fervor of the group that had drawn him in like a moth to a flame.

"Brother Felix," Ovidius called out to him, "come forward."

Felix hesitated for a moment before stepping into the flickering candlelight. His heart raced as he stood in front of the other members, who looked upon him with a mixture of sympathy and expectation.

"Your love for Quintus has led you astray," Ovidius said with a hint of condescension. "But we are here to guide you back to the righteous path."

"Quintus is lost," Caius interjected, his scarred face twisted into a scowl. "He refuses to see the truth, but you, Felix, have been given another chance."

"Indeed," Ovidius agreed, turning his piercing gaze to Felix. "The One does not approve of your sinful past, but through our teachings, you can be saved. Lucia, come forth."

A young woman stepped out from the shadows, her raven-black hair cascading down her back, her eyes filled with an intense devotion. She reached out a hand towards Felix, who hesitated before finally accepting it.

"Through this union, you will be purified," Ovidius declared. "You must let go of your love for Quintus and embrace the love that the One has ordained for you."

"Quintus only brought me pain," Felix whispered, his voice filled with anguish. "Maybe... maybe this is the right path."

"Indeed, it is," Ovidius said, a satisfied smile crossing his lips. "Embrace your future, Felix, and let go of your past."

As Felix looked into Lucia's eyes, he saw an unwavering devotion that mirrored his own growing faith in the Followers' cause. He knew that letting go of Quintus would be difficult, but the promise of salvation and belonging was too strong to resist.

"Very well," he murmured, squeezing Lucia's hand. "I will do as the One commands."

"Excellent," Ovidius said, clapping his hands together. "Now, let us pray for our brother Felix's journey towards redemption."

The cult members bowed their heads, chanting softly in unison as Felix closed his eyes, tears streaming down his face. Deep inside, he knew that there would always be a part of him that loved Quintus, but the lure of the Followers had proven too powerful to deny. And so, he vowed to cast aside his past and embrace the radical beliefs that would shape his future.

"There is another who has seduced Quintus," Felix said sadly. "A new prophet has come to town, and he has predicted great doom to fall on Pompeii."

"Then he is a false prophet!" Ovidius roared. His voice was commanding and stern, demanding absolute obedience from his Followers. "We must remain vigilant," he warned, his piercing eyes scanning the room. "Our enemies are everywhere, seeking to destroy us and our faith."

"But the people believe him! His words are convincing."

"Who is this new prophet?"

"He is called Iosephus. He dwells in the house of Quintus' father, Salvius."

"Then bring him here" bellowed Caius, his muscular build and scarred face a testament to his aggressive demeanor. "We will show him the wrath of the One!"

"Silence, Caius," Ovidius snapped, his voice cold and unyielding. "Violence is not the answer. We must trust in the guidance of the One and the teachings of our prophet Paulus."

Caius bowed his head, seething with barely contained rage. The other members of the cult exchanged nervous glances, their fear of retribution for disobedience palpable. Felix, the newest recruit, stood at the edge of the gathering, his heart pounding in his chest. He couldn't help but think about Quintus, thoughts he knew were bad. Despite their newfound distance, the bond between them still lingered, a painful reminder of what they'd been forced to relinquish.

"Let us commence our ritual," said Ovidius, raising his hands to the heavens. The Followers began to chant in hushed voices, their words blending together in a haunting melody that echoed through the temple's dark recesses. As they chanted, they traced the symbol of the icthus on their foreheads, a gesture of faith and loyalty to the One. Felix hesitated for a moment, his hand trembling before he finally completed the ritual, feeling the weight of his decision settle upon him.

"Brothers and sisters," Ovidius proclaimed, "we must stand united in our devotion to the One. We cannot allow ourselves to be swayed by doubt or temptation."

His gaze fell on Felix and Quintus, their eyes briefly meeting before they quickly looked away. The tension between them was almost palpable, a silent battle that threatened to undermine the unity of the Followers.

"Remember," Ovidius continued, "our salvation lies in our obedience to the teachings of the One and our prophet Paulus. Stray from the path, and you will find only darkness and despair."

As the cult members bowed their heads in somber agreement, Felix couldn't help but wonder if he had made the right choice.

The echoes of his past with Quintus tugged at his heart, but the promise of redemption and belonging within the cult held him captive. Only time would tell if the path he had chosen would lead to salvation or destruction.

The chanting of the cult members filled the temple, their voices low and reverent as they recited the sacred words passed down to them by their prophet, Paulus. The eerie silence between each verse was broken only by the soft rustle of robes and the steady drip of water from the temple's leaking roof.

As the meeting progressed, a subtle shift in the atmosphere occurred. The shadows seemed darker, the candles burned lower, and the oppressive weight of secrecy intensified.

"Brothers and sisters," Ovidius intoned, his voice heavy with the gravity of their purpose, "we must remain ever vigilant against those who would threaten our faith."

A murmur of agreement rippled through the congregation, followed by a sudden hush as the doors of the temple creaked open. The sound sent a wave of panic through the assembled Followers, their eyes darting towards the entrance, where a hooded figure hesitated just beyond the threshold.

"Who dares intrude upon our sacred gathering?" Ovidius demanded, his voice thundering through the temple.

"Reveal yourself, or face the wrath of the One!" Caius roared, brandishing his sword menacingly.

The figure stepped forward, pulling back the hood to reveal a terrified young woman. Her eyes widened as she took in the sight of the imposing cult members, their faces shrouded by shadows and the flickering candlelight.

"Please, I mean no harm," she stammered, her voice trembling. "I was curious about your group and wanted to learn more."

"Curiosity can be a dangerous thing," Ovidius warned, his gaze cold and unyielding. "We do not take kindly to outsiders."

"Then let me join you," the woman pleaded, desperation etched onto her features. "I want to find the truth, just like you."

"Your intentions may be pure," Caius sneered, "but how can we trust you? How do we know you're not a spy sent to destroy us?"

"Perhaps she is here for a reason," Felix interjected, his voice soft yet firm. "Maybe the One led her to us."

The cult members exchanged wary glances, their uncertainty palpable. Ovidius studied the woman for a moment before nodding slowly.

"Very well," he conceded. "But know this: if you betray our faith or our trust, there will be no mercy."

As the woman joined the congregation, offering her solemn vow of loyalty, the Followers resumed their chanting, the eerie silence once again settling over the ancient temple. But even as they raised their voices in unified worship, an undercurrent of unease persisted, a reminder that their world was forever balanced on the edge of a knife.

The tension in the air was palpable, like a living creature coiled and ready to strike. Ovidius stood tall at the center of the congregation, his imposing figure casting an ominous shadow on the crumbling walls of the ancient temple. The flickering candlelight danced across his face as he observed his Followers with piercing eyes that seemed to see into their very souls.

"Your commitment to our cause is commendable," Ovidius began, his powerful voice resonating through the eerie silence. "But let us not forget our purpose here. We are bound by our faith in the One and our loyalty to each other."

His gaze lingered on Caius, whose scarred visage betrayed a hint of defiance. The tension between the leader and his second in command was no secret among the Followers; whispers of dissent had spread like wildfire, fueled by Caius's aggressive demeanor and propensity for violence.

"Ovidius, we must protect our faith and our brothers and sisters at all costs," Caius growled, his muscular build taut with barely restrained anger. "If that means shedding blood, then so be it."

"Indeed, Caius," Ovidius replied, his tone measured and controlled. "But we must also remember the teachings of Paulus, our prophet. We cannot allow ourselves to become consumed by hatred or vengeance."

As the two men locked eyes, the other members of the cult

shifted nervously, acutely aware of the precarious balance of power within their ranks. They knew all too well the consequences of disobedience—the heavy hand of retribution that would swiftly descend upon those who dared to defy their leader.

In the midst of this turmoil, Felix found himself torn between his new allegiance to the Followers and the lingering love he still harbored for Quintus. He had been persuaded to abandon their relationship in favor of a more 'acceptable' union with Lucia, but the memory of their shared passion haunted him like a specter, refusing to be banished.

"Let us pray," Ovidius intoned, breaking the tense silence that had settled over the congregation. They bowed their heads in unison, their voices joining together.

"Father in Heaven, holy is your name," they began, their words echoing through the ancient temple. "May your kingdom come, may your your will be done, in terra and in caelum..."

As they continued their recitation, the air seemed to thicken with emotion, the fervor of their devotion almost palpable. For a moment, the divisions among them were forgotten—united by their faith and their determination to survive against all odds.

"Forgive us our sins, as we forgive those who sin against us," their voices filled the shadows, their eyes closed and heads bowed low. "And lead us not into temptation, but deliver us from evil..."

"... and for our sworn enemy, Saul of Tarsus, who has brought nothing but suffering and death to our people." Caius took over, "May he be struck down with the most painful of afflictions. May his flesh be torn from his bones, and his entrails spilled forth like an unending torrent. Let his screams echo through the Empire until they pierce the very heavens themselves, so that even the Father may bear witness to his agony. May he beg for death, yet find no relief, and when finally his spirit is ripped from his mangled corpse, let it be cast into the darkest depths of hell, there to suffer for all eternity." With a final, seething rage, he added, "Amen."

"Am... Amen," Ovidius murmured, his voice barely audible, but just loud enough for the others to hear. He glanced around the circle as if searching for any sign that his authority had been undermined by Caius's outburst.

As the meeting dispersed and the Followers began to make their way back into the night, Ovidius lingered behind, his eyes distant and troubled. There was something he was keeping from the others—a secret that threatened to tear their fragile alliance apart. He was wise to keep it from them.

* * *

On a pleasant summer evening, Salvius and I sat on a plush couch and sipping wine in the atrium. The room was illuminated by flickering oil lamps that glow warmly over the frescoes adorning the walls.

"Ah, Io! Come, join me," Salvius had beckoned, pouring another glass of wine and gesturing for me to take a seat opposite him. "It's been quite a day, hasn't it?"

I nodded and took the proffered glass, grateful for the opportunity to discuss the unsettling matters that weighed on my mind. "Indeed, it has been an eventful day. How are you faring, Salvius?"

"Truth be told, I'm concerned for Quintus. He's always been headstrong and impulsive, but this newfound fascination with Felix and his beliefs... it worries me." Salvius swirled his wine thoughtfully. "Before all this, I held Felix in high regard. He was a good friend to my son, and I never imagined he'd become involved with such a group."

"Groups like these can have a powerful allure," I said carefully, choosing my words so as not to reveal too much. "Sometimes, they can sweep people off their feet before they realize what they've gotten into."

Salvius raised an eyebrow. "You speak as if you know them well."

"Perhaps not these specific individuals," I admitted, "but I've heard tales of groups who claim to offer salvation, only to bring about ruin in the end. Their members become trapped, unable to escape the web of deceit they've been caught in."

"Like the myth of Arachne, who challenged Minerva and was transformed into a spider, forever condemned to weave her intricate designs?" Salvius mused, a shadow of sadness crossing his face. "I pray that Quintus will not find himself ensnared by such a fate."

"Sometimes, all one needs is a guiding hand to lead them back to the right path," I offered, trying to provide some comfort.

"Perhaps you are right, Io." Salvius drained the last of his wine and set the empty glass on the table. "For now, let us hope that Quintus can find his way out of this tangled mess."

I nodded in agreement, my thoughts once again turning to the cult whose doctrine seemed so familiar. The intensity of their convictions, combined with the tragic stories of similar groups from my own time, sent a shiver down my spine. What sort of future lay ahead for Felix, Quintus, and the rest of the Followers?

"Time will tell what comes of this," I murmured, taking a sip of my wine and hoping against hope that they would find their way back to the light before it was too late.

The night wind carried the scent of blooming jasmine through the open doors of the villa, mingling with the aroma of the wine in my cup. I took a sip, savoring its rich, fruity flavor as I gazed out at the moonlit garden where shadows danced among the marble statues and well-tended flower beds.

"Something troubles you, Io," Salvius observed, his voice tinged with concern.

"Merely pondering the paths that life takes us on," I replied, trying to keep my worries hidden from him. "Sometimes they lead us to unexpected destinations."

"Indeed." Salvius nodded, refilling his cup. "And sometimes, those destinations can change our entire perception of the world."

"Like the Followers, for instance," I said cautiously, testing the waters. "Their beliefs challenge the very foundations of our society. They're at odds with everything we've been taught."

"True," Salvius conceded with a sigh. "But it's not only their beliefs that worry me. It's the risk. Their religion has been outlawed since Gaius Germanicus was Emperor."

"Ahh, good old Gaius Germanicus," I smirked, raising my glass. "Are you daft, Iosephus? He was a monster!"

"Of course he was," I said, trying to save face. You see, history remembers Gaius Germanicus by a different name: Caligula. "I was just being sarcastic."

"Don't even jest about that madman." He sighed and sipped his wine. He seemed to want to change the subject, as if talking about Caligula might bring him back to life. "The unrest in Judea is our own fault, I tell you. They should never have executed their 'messiah' or whatever they call him. It only made him a martyr."

"Let me guess," I said, stroking my chin. This story was sounding way too familiar. "This happened in Jerusalem, right?"

"Yes, and the governor lost his head for it." Salvius sipped again. "Judea has been a thorn in our side for over a century, and they just aren't worth the trouble. Even their land is useless. They live in a desert next to a poisonous sea." He sipped again and shook his head. "We thought Masada would be the end of it, but now we have this new upstart cult stabbing at the heart of Rome itself."

I smiled knowingly, not about to tell Salvius that this upstart cult would someday be the official religion of Rome, and they'd rule most of the world someday. "A wise man where I come from once said, never underestimate the power of stupid people in large groups."

"A wise man indeed," Salvius nodded, smiling and taking another sip.

"Perhaps they believe that the world they create will be better than the one we live in now," I mused, thinking back on the cult meeting I had witnessed. The passion in their eyes and the fervor of their prayers were both fascinating and terrifying.

"Maybe," Salvius agreed, slowly sipping his wine. "But such drastic change rarely comes without a price. And I fear that price may be too high for some to bear."

"Like Quintus?" I ventured, watching as his expression darkened.

"Exactly. He has always been headstrong and impulsive, but this… is unlike anything he's ever done. I can't help but wonder if there's more to it than meets the eye."

"Perhaps there is something about the Followers that we don't yet understand," I suggested, my mind racing with possibilities. "Something that could make them valuable allies, or dangerous enemies."

"Or perhaps," Salvius said quietly, his gaze distant, "the true nature of their intentions lies somewhere in between."

We fell into silence, each lost in our own thoughts as the wind whispered through the garden and the moon continued its slow journey across the sky. The world seemed to hold its breath, waiting for us to decide—to choose a side in a battle far larger than any one person.

As I looked into the depths of my wine cup, reflections of the past and shadows of the future swirled together, and I knew that the choice I made would shape not only my destiny but the fate of all those whose lives were entwined with mine.

"So tell me, Iosephus," Salvius noticed, "you seem to be getting rather close to Marcus."

I smiled awkwardly. "Yes, I have. Does this disturb you... I mean, he is your property..."

"Only as a favor to his family," Salvius explained. "They had dreams of Marcus becoming a gladiator, but he didn't work out. He's a loving, gentle soul who couldn't bring him to harm another human being, so his family sold him into slavery. I think they wanted to sell him into prostitution, but I made him a house servant instead." He sipped his wine and smiled. "It makes my heart glad to see he has found someone to love."

"Time will tell," I murmured, steeling myself for the challenges ahead. "Time will tell."

CHAPTER IX

As I stood by the window, I couldn't help but feel a twinge of sadness in my heart. The sky was ablaze with brilliant hues of orange and crimson, casting an ethereal glow over the city of Pompeii. I sensed Quintus approaching and turned to face him.

"Quintus," I said softly, acknowledging his presence.

"Io," he replied, his voice cracking slightly as he tried to maintain his composure. "I can't stop thinking about Felix."

I sighed. "I know you're hurt, but Felix made his choice, Quintus."

"Did he really?" Quintus challenged, his eyes glistening with unshed tears. "Or was it the Followers who made the choice for him? Just like they made the 'choice' of Lucia for him?"

I hesitated, unsure of what to say. "I don't have all the answers, Quintus, but perhaps the upcoming Saturnalia festival will help lift your spirits."

"Maybe," he muttered, unconvinced.

* * *

A few days later, we found ourselves at Septimus Caerellius' annual celebration on the eve of Saturnalia. As the town magistrate and father of Felix, Septimus spared no expense to entertain the elite of Pompeii. Salvius, Livia, Quintus, and I were among the guests, dressed in our finest attire. The air was thick with the scent of exotic perfumes, and the sound of laughter rang through the opulently decorated halls. Salvius was feeling quite merry already, and I was smiling politely and nodding as he told what was an old joke where I came from. "So a man from Pompeii has come to Rome, and walking on the streets was drawing everyone's attention, being a real double of the emperor Augustus. The emperor, having brought him to the palace, looks at him and then asks, 'Tell me, young man, did your mother come to Rome anytime?'" He sipped his wine and chuckled to himself before delivering the punchline. "The man replies, 'She never did. But my father frequently was here.'"

After two thousand years, I still don't get it. But I still laughed anyway, just to be polite.

"Ah, there you are!" Septimus greeted us warmly. "Come, join the festivities!"

"Thank you, Septimus," I replied, forcing a smile. My heart ached for Quintus, who couldn't hide his disappointment over Felix's absence.

"Where is your son, Felix?" asked Salvius, ever the diplomat. "He's missed among us."

"Ah, Felix," sighed Septimus, his jovial demeanor faltering. "He's been so distant lately. I don't know what's going on with him." He shook his head, unaware of the true reason behind his son's withdrawal.

As we mingled among the guests, I couldn't help but feel a sense of foreboding. Quintus' heartbreak weighed heavily on me, and I wished there was some way to mend the rift between him and Felix. But for now, all I could do was be there for my friend and hope that the joy of Saturnalia would bring some solace to his wounded soul.

As the evening's festivities continued, I found myself at the center of attention. Guests thronged around me, eager to ask questions and seek my advice on all manner of topics. From history to philosophy, politics to love, it seemed as if no subject was too obscure or too personal for them to broach.

"Tell us, Io," said a matron with an ostentatious display of jewelry, "what do you think of the current fashion trends in Rome? Are we in Pompeii hopelessly behind the times?"

"Ah, dear lady," I replied with a charming smile, "Rome may set the trends, but Pompeii will always be known for its unique flair and sense of style."

Laughter rippled through the crowd, and I noticed that even Quintus seemed to be enjoying himself for the moment.

"Come, Io," she beckoned. "I have someone you simply must meet." She led me to a distinguished-looking older man with tight curly hair and a beard that hugged his jawline. He looked vaguely familiar.

"Io," Octavia smiled graciously. "This is Gaius Plinius Secundus."

"Please," the old man added, "call me Pliny."

Huh?! I stared at the stranger in shock, suddenly realizing who he was. Pliny the Elder! "Holy shit!" I let slip in English.

Pliny looked at me strangely. "What did you say?"

"Uh… it's an old Celtic blessing." I recovered my composure and nodded politely. I felt like a fawning fanboy. "I am so honored to meet you, Pliny. I've read so much of your work."

"Then you have me at a disadvantage, sir. What is your name and where do you come from?

"I am Iosephus Andrius. I come from… Alexandria."

The elder's brow furrowed. "Which one?"

"Uh… the one I was born in." I shrugged awkwardly. "Please, call me Io."

The old man smiled for the first time since I met him. "And you may call me Pliny… though it is also my nephew's name. He's around here somewhere." No way! Pliny the Elder and Pliny the Younger at the same party? History teachers have dreams about things like this… though we're usually naked in the dreams. "What brings you to Pompeii?"

"The city has always fascinated me. Especially Vesuvius. Have you ever seen a more handsome mountain?"

"You should see Etna in Sicily," the Elder bragged. "It is the forge of Vulcan. I have seen fire and smoke rising from it. It is truly an awesome sight—if you can stand the reek of sulfur."

The irony. Oh, how it burned. "I have seen many fire mountains in my travels." I really, really wanted to change the subject. "Um... how do you manage to write on so many topics? You have written about everything from astronomy to zoology."

"It is not easy, I admit. I have to read a lot of books, observe a lot of phenomena, and consult a lot of experts. I also have to organize my material carefully and choose the best words to express my thoughts. I have seen sights you would not believe. I have seen the moon turn to blood and the sun turn black!"

"An inspiring sight, is it not?"

"You have seen it, too?"

"Last year, uh, in my homeland." Also, not a lie, except I had driven to Illinois to watch the eclipse last year—and last year was 1,939 years from now.

"Have you read Plutarch?" asked Pliny. "I don't know if you've ever heard of him, he's Greek."

"The name is not strange to me," I nodded,

"He has a most intriguing theory," Pliny told me. "He believes that it is Selene seducing Helios that causes it to turn black. Of course, we know them as Apollo and Diana."

"A most interesting theory." The thought of the god of the sun getting it on with the goddess of the moon brought a smile to my face. I was almost tempted to explain to Pliny exactly what an eclipse is and why Plutarch had the right idea, but that would be a major violation of the Prime Directive. It was time to change the subject again. "How are you able to write so much? How does your hand not cramp?"

"I make use of every moment. I write when I travel, when I eat, when I bathe, even when I sleep. I have a scribe who follows me everywhere and takes notes of what I say."

"Do you ever relax or have fun?"

"Of course, I do. I enjoy the company of my friends and family. I also like to visit the theater and the baths. And sometimes I go on expeditions to see new places and things."

"Like Pompeii?"

"Yes, like Pompeii. Why do you ask?"

"Oh, no reason. Just curious."

"You seem very nervous, Io. Is there something you want to tell me?"

Like what? That Vesuvius was a ticking time bomb, a fire mountain like Etna but packing a much more powerful punch? That he was going to die trying to save the people of Pompeii when it erupted? "No, no, nothing at all," I lied. "Everything is fine."

"*Salve, amice,*" Pliny the Elder said to a friend as he approached. "I was just telling this young man about my latest work on natural history. He is Io, a scholar from Alexandria." He turned to me. "Io, this is my good friend, Publius Cornelius Tacitus."

Tacitus? *The* Tacitus? I was officially impressed with Septimus. He had the most interesting friends. "Wow. I've read all your work, too." Flippantly, I asked, "Is Seneca here too?"

Tacitus looked at me with a shocked expression. "If you'd really read my work, you'd know that Seneca died thirteen years ago."

Oops. "I've been traveling extensively," I said, trying to recover. I just made a fool of myself in front of two of the greatest writers of the Roman Empire! "I may not be caught up on your more recent work."

Tacitus nodded. "So, you are from Alexandria? That is a great city of learning. Which one do you mean? There are several, I hear."

Pliny laughed and said, "The one he was born in, of course!" he laughed, slapping me on the back. "Don't be so curious, Tacitus. You are always looking for secrets and scandals in your histories."

Tacitus smiled wryly and said, "And you are always looking for wonders and marvels in your natural history. Tell me, Pliny, have you found any new animals or plants to describe?"

Pliny's eyes lit up, and he said, "As a matter of fact, I have. Just recently, I received a letter from a friend in Africa who told me about a strange beast he saw. It had the body of a horse, the head of a lion, and the tail of a scorpion. He called it a hippalektryon."

Tacitus raised his eyebrows and said, "A hippalektryon? That sounds like a fabulous creature from Greek mythology. Are you sure your friend was not joking?"

Pliny shook his head and said, "No, no, he was very serious. He even sent me a sketch of the animal. Look, here it is." He took out a parchment from his tunic and showed it to Tacitus and Io.

Io looked at the drawing and suppressed a laugh. It looked like a child's attempt to draw a monster. He wondered if Pliny's friend had made it up or if he had seen some kind of hybrid animal that resembled a hippalektryon.

"What do you think of it, Io?" Pliny asked.

I hesitated and said, "It is very... interesting. I have never seen anything like it before."

Pliny nodded and said, "Neither have I. That is why I am eager to learn more about it. Perhaps I will travel to Africa someday and see it for myself."

Tacitus shook his head and said, "One of these days, Plinius, your thirst for adventure will be your death."

I stood there smiling and biting my tongue.

Pliny waved his hand and said, "Nonsense, Tacitus. The world is full of wonders and discoveries that are waiting to be explored and explained. That is why I write my natural history, to share my knowledge with others."

Tacitus sighed and said, "And that is why I write my histories, to warn others of the follies and crimes of the past."

The two friends looked at each other and smiled. They had known each other for a long time and respected each other's work, even if they did not agree on everything.

They were interrupted by the arrival of Pliny's nephew, Pliny the Younger. He was a young man of seventeen who had accompanied his uncle to Pompeii for the summer.

"Uncle," he said impatiently, "can we go now? The party is over and I am bored."

Pliny looked at him and said, "Not so fast, nephew. You have not met our friend Tacitus yet. He is a famous historian and a senator. And this is Io, a most amazing scholar."

Pliny the Younger glanced at us and said, "*Salve*." Then he turned to his uncle and said, "Can we go now?"

Pliny sighed and said, "Very well, nephew. But you should show more interest in history and literature. They are important for your education and career." He turned to me. "Tell me, Iosephus, have you any words of wisdom to pass on to my nephew?"

I suppose I could have told the kid to stop his uncle from coming to Pompeii's rescue, but that would be changing history. If there are rules of time travel, that's probably the Prime Directive. Still, Pliny expected me to say something profound to his nephew, so I gave him a firm pat on the shoulder and smiled. *"Carpe diem."*

Pliny the Younger rolled his eyes and said, "Whatever you say, uncle." He took his uncle's arm and led him away.

Tacitus watched them go and turned to me. "He is a bright boy, but he has no patience for learning. He prefers to spend his time on games."

"I've known many like him," I smiled, thinking of the students in Minneapolis he reminded me of. "He is young. He will change when he grows older. I'm sure he will follow in your footsteps and be a great historian himself."

Tacitus shrugged and said, "Maybe. Or maybe he will remain the same. Who knows what the future holds?"

I felt a chill run down my spine as I heard those words. I knew what the future held for Pompeii and its inhabitants. I knew that in less than a year, Vesuvius would erupt and bury the city in ash and lava. I knew that Pliny the Elder would die trying to mount a rescue mission and that his apathetic young nephew would be left to tell the story to Tacitus.

Remember the Prime Directive, Joe.

I looked at Tacitus and said, "Who knows, indeed?" As our talk continued, I found myself walking a tightrope of discretion, carefully choosing my words so as not to reveal anything about the future. I knew the fates of all of them, some terrible, and I couldn't bear the thought of inadvertently leading any of these great men to their untimely deaths. But the thought of making a major change to history—like preventing the death of Pliny the Elder—could have historical repercussions that would ripple through time. Even in my own time, science fiction writers could only speculate about how such a paradox could ripple through time and space. Just thinking about it gave me a headache. "Ah, well," I hedged, feeling the weight of my knowledge bearing down on me, "the world is full of mysteries, and sometimes it's best to simply appreciate them for what they are."

"Spoken like a true philosopher," Tacitus remarked, raising his cup in a toast. "To the unknown and the eternal pursuit of wisdom!"

I took my leave of them to get another glass of wine. They were engaged in a heated debate about the social problems of the empire. Pliny argued that the rich should be taxed more to help feed the poor and prevent riots. Tacitus disagreed, saying that such a policy would only encourage laziness and corruption.

They noticed me standing nearby and asked for my opinion.

"Excuse me, young man," Pliny said. "You seem to be a man of learning and culture. What do you think of our discussion?"

"Yes, please share your thoughts with us," Tacitus said. "We value your perspective."

I was caught off guard and had no idea what to say. "The needs of the many," I said without thinking, "outweigh the needs of the few."

They looked at me with curiosity and admiration. "That is very noble of you," Tacitus said. "But do you not think that the rich have earned their wealth by their own merit and deserve to enjoy it?"

"I think that everyone deserves to enjoy their wealth," I said, trying to sound diplomatic. "But not at the expense of others who are suffering."

"So you would take from the rich and give to the poor?" Pliny asked.

"I would not take anything by force," I said. "But I would encourage generosity and compassion."

"And how would you do that?" Tacitus asked.

"I would... I would appeal to their reason and morality," I said, struggling to find an answer.

"Reason and morality?" Pliny repeated. "Those are rare qualities in these times."

"Indeed they are," Tacitus agreed. "But perhaps you are right. Perhaps we should listen to your philosophy more often."

I felt relieved that they bought it.

I decided to end the conversation and leave the party before I made any more blunders. I thanked them for their hospitality and bid them farewell. *"Longa vita et bene."*

Oh, the irony; I just told Pliny the Elder to live long and prosper—in Latin! Sadly, he would do neither.

"Your words honor us," Pliny nodded.

"It is a blessing," I said, amused that being a sci-fi nerd made me sound so smart to these people. "A blessing from Vulcan," I said, trying hard not to laugh.

"Vulcan? The god of fire?" Pliny asked.

"Yes, yes, the god of fire," I said, feeling nervous. "He is very wise and benevolent—and, uh, logical."

They smiled and repeated the gesture. Well, they tried. Not everyone can do the Vulcan greeting. It took me years of practice. *"Longa vita et bene,"* said Tacitus.

"Longa vita et bene," Pliny added.

* * *

As I bid farewell to the great writers, my mind still reeling about how epic that experience was, my thoughts turned to the upcoming Saturnalia celebration at Domus Marcelli. I couldn't have been more excited for Saturnalia. It was going to be my first time celebrating this ancient Roman festival in honor of Saturn, the god of agriculture and time. My research had told me that it was a week of fun and freedom, where everything was turned upside down. No work, no school, no rules! Just feasting, gambling, singing, and exchanging gifts with friends and family. I had already bought some wax candles and clay figurines to give away. I'd also heard that slaves got to enjoy the festivities too, and even were served by their masters. How crazy was that? I wondered what else would happen during this carnival of joy and merriment. Maybe I'd even get to wear a colorful robe and a funny hat. I hoped Saturn had blessed us with a good harvest next year. He must have been happy to see us having such a good time!

The house was already a whirl of activity as preparations were underway. Garlands of ivy and laurel festooned the walls and doorways, and candles flickered in every corner, casting warm golden light on the opulent furnishings.

"Ah, Io!" Quintus greeted me with a grin as he adjusted a wreath around a marble statue's head. "Io, Saturnalia! You're just in time to help me with this stubborn thing!"

"Io, Saturnalia!" I replied, stepping over to lend a hand. "Of course, I'll help; I wouldn't want to miss out on any of the festivities."

Once we'd secured the decoration, Quintus led me into the *triclinium* where an impressive spread of food awaited us. The table groaned beneath the weight of roasted meats, olives, cheeses, and sweet honey cakes. Goblets filled with spiced wine awaited our lips, while slaves scurried about, putting the finishing touches on the banquet.

"Fabius has truly outdone himself this year," I mused, admiring the culinary delights.

"Indeed," Quintus agreed, plucking a grape from a nearby plate and popping it into his mouth. "Though I must confess, I'm looking forward to the games more than anything else."

"Ah, yes," I said, recalling the various activities that would be taking place throughout the house. There would be dancing in the atrium, singing in the peristyle, and even a friendly game of knucklebones in the *tablinum* for those who fancied a bit of gambling.

Quintus sampled a cube of meat and smiled as he swallowed. "Try the lion," he said, "it's delicious!"

Lion? "Uh, maybe later." I might have tried it if I only had the nerve.

"Speaking of which," Quintus continued, "Father and Mother are leaving soon for their holiday, so we'll have free rein of the house."

"Sounds like fun," I replied, watching as Salvius and Livia made their farewells to the household staff, their dog, Canno, wagging his tail excitedly at their side. I had already figured out that his name was the Latin equivalent of doggo. That was cute. "I hope they have a lovely trip."

"Indeed," Quintus agreed. "Now, let's get this celebration started!"

As the last echoes of Salvius and Livia's voices faded down the street, the house erupted into merriment. I found myself lost in the revelry, dancing with the slaves, singing bawdy songs, and even trying my hand at knucklebones. The wine flowed freely, its warmth spreading through me as I threw myself wholeheartedly into the festivities.

"Is it always like this?" I wondered aloud, breathless from dancing.

"Only during Saturnalia!" Quintus laughed, clapping me on the back. "It's a time for us all to forget our troubles and simply enjoy life."

"Then let's make the most of it," I grinned, raising my goblet in a toast. "To Saturnalia, and all the joy it brings!"

"Io, Saturnalia!" Quintus echoed, clinking his cup against mine before we both drank deeply, embracing the spirit of the season.

The *exoleti*, dressed in brightly-colored silks and wearing headdresses of gold thread, arrived at the palace gates well before sunset. They were given wristbands that provided access to the full week of festivities; after all, this was the only time of the year where differences between classes could be set aside so everyone could enjoy fine food, music, and dance. Tiberius strummed a lyre he brought with him, accompanied by clapping hands and laughter from the revelers.

As the night progressed, inhibitions were slowly released and clothing was discarded. The air was intoxicatingly sweet with wine, incense, and desire. Bodies moved in a kind of dance, letting go of their worries while soft laughter filled the room. And behind closed doors, the sounds of pleasure spilled out. "Come on, Io," Quintus urged, tugging me into a dimly lit room where Marcus and several other men were already engaged in passionate embraces. I hesitated for a moment, then decided that if I was going to experience Saturnalia in its full glory, I needed to cast aside my inhibitions.

I joined Marcus, our lips meeting hungrily as we pressed against each other, our hands exploring the contours of our bodies. The sensation of his skin against mine sent a shiver down my spine, igniting a fire within me that demanded satisfaction. As we kissed, I became aware of Antonius, Petrus, and Tiberius joining us, their firm hands caressing my shoulders, chest, and thighs.

"Let yourself go, Io," Marcus whispered into my ear, nipping playfully at my lobe. "Tonight is about pleasure and indulgence."

My senses were overwhelmed, intoxicated by the taste of his kiss, the warmth of his breath on my skin, and the intoxicating scent of his body. I surrendered myself to the sensations, allowing my desire to guide me as I explored new depths of passion with these beautiful men.

Quintus, too, succumbed to the hedonism of the night, his eyes dark with lust as he watched the writhing mass of naked flesh before him. With a grin, he shed his clothes and joined the fray, his muscular body a welcome addition to the tangled web of limbs and mouths.

In the parlor, our passions reached a fever pitch, the air charged with electricity as we gave ourselves over to our most primal instincts. The room was a kaleidoscope of entwined bodies, each taking and giving pleasure in equal measure. The sound of flesh slapping against flesh, the moans and cries of ecstasy, and the heavy panting of exertion filled the space, creating a symphony of decadence.

As I reveled in the debauchery, a nagging thought tugged at the edge of my consciousness, a sense of unease that something unexpected might happen—a sudden arrival or a simmering conflict that could shatter this moment of hedonistic bliss. I tried to push the feeling aside, focusing instead on the pleasure coursing through my veins, but it lingered like a shadow, threatening to darken the festivities.

"Enjoy yourself, Io," Quintus called out breathlessly, his eyes locked onto mine as he thrust into another man. "Forget your worries for one night."

I nodded, forcing a smile as I attempted to lose myself once more in the abandon of Saturnalia. But deep down, I couldn't shake the feeling that our revelry would soon be interrupted, and the consequences would be anything but festive.

The door to the parlor creaked open, and I tore my gaze away from the carnal embrace of Marcus and Tiberius to see who was intruding on our Saturnalia celebration. My heart skipped a beat as Felix Caerellius, Quintus's former lover, stood hesitantly in the doorway. His eyes were wide with shock, and his jaw clenched as he took in the tableau of drunken naked men before him.

Felix's clothing was uncharacteristically disheveled, as if he had been in a hurry; his tunic was hastily fastened, leaving it uneven at the hem, and his sandals were scuffed with dirt. The torchlight flickered across his face, casting shadows that emphasized the tension etched in his handsome features.

"My god," Felix muttered under his breath, his voice barely audible above the raucous moans and laughter filling the room. From his perspective, the scene must have been overwhelming: a sea of writhing bodies, the air thick with the scent of wine and sweat, and the floor littered with discarded cups and plates of half-eaten food—an orgy of hedonistic excess.

"Quintus," Felix called out, his voice wavering as his gaze locked onto the man he once loved. "What… what is this?"

"Saturnalia, my friend! Join us!" Quintus slurred, raising a cup of wine in toast before downing it in one gulp.

"Is this what you've become?" Felix asked bitterly, his eyes darting around the room, taking in the various acts being performed with an expression of thinly veiled disgust. His chest heaved with barely-contained anger, and I could see the muscles in his neck tense as he struggled to maintain his composure amid the debauchery.

"Come now, Felix," I interjected, attempting to diffuse the situation. "It's just a celebration, a chance to let loose and forget our troubles for one night. There's no harm in it."

"Is that what you think?" Felix retorted, his gaze narrowing as he focused on me. I could see the gears turning in his mind, searching for anything to condemn the chaos unfolding before him.

"Enough," Quintus snapped, staggering to his feet and crossing the room to confront his former lover. "Felix, if you cannot accept who I am now, then perhaps it is best that you leave."

Silence hung heavily in the air for a moment, broken only by the heavy breathing and muffled moans of those still entwined in their carnal pursuits. Felix stared at Quintus, his eyes filled with a mixture of sadness, anger, and disbelief.

"Very well," Felix said finally, his voice cold and hard as he turned to leave. "Enjoy your celebration, Quintus. I hope it brings you the happiness you so desperately seek."

My own thoughts churned with uncertainty and unease, wondering whether this brief brush with conflict was merely a taste of what was yet to come.

In a haze of wine and desire, I watched as Quintus stumbled over to Felix, his arm outstretched in an attempt at camaraderie. "Fe-Felix," he slurred, nearly tripping over his own feet in his inebriation. "Don't be like this! Come, join us! It's *Saturnalia!*"

The room seemed to grow quieter as the revelers paused their activities, suddenly aware of the tension that had tightened like a vice around Felix and Quintus. It felt like the moment before a storm, when the air is charged with electricity and the world holds its breath.

"Shame, Felix?" Quintus retorted, his voice gaining strength as he squared his shoulders. "Why should we be ashamed? We are celebrating life, love, and each other! If you cannot understand that, then perhaps you do not belong here after all."

"Perhaps not," Felix whispered, shaking his head as he took a step back from Quintus. He looked around the room once more, his gaze lingering on me for a heartbeat before darting away. "I had hoped that you would see reason, Quintus. That you would remember what we once had and choose to follow a different path."

"Things have changed, Felix," Quintus replied, his voice softer now as he reached out toward his former lover, only to let his hand drop back to his side. "We've both made our choices. You chose the Followers, and I... I chose this."

"Then I pity you, Quintus," Felix murmured, his eyes filled with sorrow as he turned away. "I truly do."

As Felix left the room, I could see the hurt and confusion that simmered beneath Quintus's determined facade. We had all been so caught up in the revelry of Saturnalia that we had forgotten, for a moment, the world beyond these walls—a world where not everyone shared our ideals or our desires.

"Quintus," I began, reaching out to place a hand on his shoulder. "Are you—"

"Let him go, Io," Quintus interrupted, his voice brittle as he attempted to smile. "He's made his choice. Now let us continue making ours."

The tension in the room seemed to hang over us like a thick fog, making it difficult to breathe. I watched as my friends tried to make sense of what had just happened, their eyes darting between Quintus and the door that Felix had slammed shut moments ago.

"Quintus," Antonius said hesitantly, placing a hand on his shoulder, "I'm so sorry about Felix. We all know how much you cared for him."

Quintus gave a bitter chuckle, trying to mask the pain in his eyes. "It's fine, really. He made his choice, and I've made mine."

"Right," Tiberius chimed in, clearly eager to move past the awkwardness. "We're here to celebrate Saturnalia, after all! Let's not dwell on those who choose not to join us."

Petrus nodded in agreement, raising his cup in a toast. "To Saturnalia, and to friendship! May our bonds only grow stronger in the face of adversity!"

"Here, here!" Marcus added, his voice cutting through the tense atmosphere. As if on cue, the musicians picked up their instruments once more, and the familiar melodies of the celebration filled the air.

Despite the renewed energy, I couldn't shake the feeling that something had shifted within our group dynamic. It was as if Felix's departure had left an open wound that would fester if we didn't address it properly.

"Are you alright, Io?" Gaius asked, noticing my furrowed brow.

"Fine, fine," I said with a forced smile, trying to push the thoughts away. "Just worried about Quintus, is all."

"Ah," Gaius nodded sagely. "Well, he's a strong lad. And he has all of us supporting him. He'll pull through."

"Indeed," Nuntius agreed, clapping me on the back. "Now, let's put this unpleasantness behind us and enjoy the festivities!"

With that, we threw ourselves back into the raucous celebration, trying to chase away the shadows of Felix's departure with laughter and merriment. We danced until our legs ached, drank until we were dizzy, and indulged in every pleasure Saturnalia had to offer.

"Alright, everyone," I announced as the night wore on, my voice heavy with the weight of unspoken thoughts. "Felix has made his decision, and we've made ours. Let's continue celebrating Saturnalia as it was meant to be celebrated—with joy, laughter, and love."

And so we did. We reveled in the moment, eager to forget the pain of lost love and broken friendships. For one brief, shining evening, we immersed ourselves in Saturnalia's spirit, embracing the festival's freedom and chaos.

The air was thick with passion and desire as I stepped back into the parlor, my eyes lingering over the scene of naked men entwined in each other's arms. The smell of sweat and oil filled my senses, making me shiver with delight.

"Let's not dwell on those who choose to walk away from us," I raised a toast, watching as Quintus smiled through the haze of wine and song. "Tonight, we celebrate life, love, and the bonds that hold us together."

"Io, Saturnalia!" The crowd roared in agreement, raising their cups high in the air.

"Io, Saturnalia!" I echoed, feeling a surge of warmth and camaraderie as our voices joined together in a triumphant chorus.

Marcus' gaze met mine, and he smiled, beckoning me closer to join them. His eyes seemed to promise something far more than pleasure, a knowing that we together could create something beautiful.

Without hesitation, I moved towards the others, allowing myself to be drawn into their embrace. Antonius' hands explored my body, while Tiberius' lips trailed along my neck, pressing hot kisses that sent sparks flying through my veins. My heart raced as I felt Petrus' hands grip my waist, and I let out a shuddering gasp of pleasure.

For hours we were lost in one another's touch, temptation leading us deeper and deeper into our own secret world. As dawn slowly crept up on us, I found myself lying between Marcus and Antonius, exhausted yet blissfully content.

The outside world faded away as I closed my eyes and listened to the beating of Marcus' heart against my ear, relishing the warmth of his skin against mine. Here in this moment I had found something precious that I never wanted to abandon. But soon enough reality would come knocking at our door, reminding us of what can happen when one chases after forbidden desires.

For that night, at least, we could pretend that our hearts were whole and our futures secure—and that was enough.

CHAPTER X

I awoke with the crushing sensation of an entire legion stamped-
ing through my skull, each soldier's hobnailed *caligae* trampling
across my throbbing brain. My mouth tasted like something had
crawled in and died during the night, and my eyes felt as if they
were swimming in a mixture of vinegar and sand. Blinking blear-
ily at my surroundings, I realized I was entangled in a sea of naked, slumbering bodies. The aftermath of Saturnalia celebrations
had left its mark on all of us.

"Marcus," I whispered hoarsely, nudging his shoulder. "Are you
alive?"

"By Jupiter, Io," Marcus groaned, rubbing his temples as he sat
up. "I feel like I've been run over by Caesar's chariot." He squinted at the others, still sprawled out like casualties from some de-
baucherous battle. "There are hangovers," he muttered, helping me
disentangle myself from the limbs and torsos, "and then there are
Saturnalia hangovers."

Just as we managed to free ourselves from the carnal wreckage,
Flavius appeared from the kitchen, looking irritatingly fresh and
alert. In his hands, he carried glasses of freshly squeezed tomato
juice.

"Salvius sent this," he said, handing us the juice. "He swears it's
the best cure for a hangover."

"May the gods bless you, Flavius," I mumbled, trying not to gag
at the smell. What I wouldn't give for a pot of black coffee right
now, but of course, they didn't know about coffee yet. I thought

about quipping that the tomato juice could use some vodka for a proper Bloody Mary but figured the joke would be lost on them.

"Bottoms up," Marcus grimaced, clinking his glass against mine before downing its contents in one go. I followed suit, shuddering as the juice slid down my throat, an odd mix of sweet and bitter that somehow felt both invigorating and nauseating at the same time.

"Only during Saturnalia would we willingly drink this," Marcus muttered, wiping his mouth. "I swear, it's like a rite of passage."

"Tell me about it," I agreed, forcing another sip down. I knew I had to finish it if I wanted any hope of surviving the day. But as I looked around at the other hungover partygoers, I couldn't help but feel a strange sense of camaraderie. We were all in this together, victims of our own indulgence, yet it was moments like these that made a living in Pompeii come alive for me. For one night, we had forgotten our troubles and reveled in the joy of being human, with all its messy, glorious imperfections.

"Here's to surviving another Saturnalia," I said, raising my glass to Marcus.

"Cheers," he replied weakly, clinking it against mine one more time before we both grimaced and downed the rest of our vile cure.

* * *

After finishing the last of our makeshift hangover cure, we all slowly got dressed, each movement feeling like a monumental effort. The *exoleti*, Petrus, Tiberius, and Antonius, were particularly sluggish and groaning as they put on their tunics. Quintus sat next to me, rubbing his temples and sighing deeply.

"Last night was truly a night for the ages," he said with a weak smile, trying to muster some enthusiasm.

"Indeed," I agreed, my head still feeling like a legion of Roman soldiers had decided to use it for target practice. As I scanned the room, I noticed that one person was conspicuously absent—Gaius, the procurator of Homo Domus.

Just as I was about to ask Quintus about his whereabouts, the door opened, and Gaius walked in, looking somber and composed. He cleared his throat and addressed the room.

"Master Quintus, my friends," Gaius began, his voice heavy with emotion. "I have given this much thought, and I can no longer continue working as the procurator of this establishment. My conscience has led me to become a disciple of the new faith, and I cannot reconcile my beliefs with this line of work."

Quintus's eyes widened in shock, and he struggled to find words as Gaius continued.

"Please understand, this decision was not made lightly, but I must follow my heart," Gaius said, bowing his head respectfully. "I wish you all the best, and may the—may *god* watch over you."

With that, Gaius turned and left the room, leaving us all in stunned silence.

"God?" Petrus looked confused. "Which god?"

"First, Felix," Quintus groaned, rubbing his temples. "Now Gaius. By the gods, Io—what am I going to do without a procurator? This place will fall apart!"

As Quintus's panic grew, an idea began to form in my mind. I knew that I needed a job, and although running a brothel wasn't exactly what I had envisioned for myself when I arrived in ancient Pompeii, it seemed like the best option available.

"Quintus," I said hesitantly, drawing his attention, "I might be able to help."

"What do you mean?" he asked, his eyes searching mine.

"I can take Gaius's place as procurator," I offered, feeling a mix of trepidation and excitement at the prospect. "I don't have much experience, but I'm a quick learner, and I promise I'll do everything in my power to keep this place running smoothly."

Quintus stared at me for a moment, seemingly weighing his options before finally nodding.

"Alright, Io, you've proven yourself trustworthy so far, and I honestly don't know who else to turn to," he admitted. "Let's give it a try. But understand, this is a serious responsibility."

"Of course," I replied, trying to hide my nervousness. "I won't let you down, I promise."

As we shook hands to seal the agreement, I couldn't help but wonder how on earth I was going to manage all this—but one thing was certain: life in Pompeii just got a whole lot more interesting.

* * *

A month had passed since I took on the role of procurator at the Homo Domus, and as I walked through the dimly lit hallways, I couldn't help but smile at the changes I'd managed to bring about. Admittedly, my knowledge of running a brothel was limited, but I drew upon my experience from the future and applied it to this ancient establishment.

First, I insisted on proper hygiene practices for both the workers and the clients. The *exoleti* seemed initially skeptical about the idea, but once they realized that cleaner conditions led to fewer illnesses and happier customers, they embraced it wholeheartedly. I even introduced the concept of a "bath and massage" package, where clients could enjoy a relaxing soak in the hot baths before their chosen service. It quickly became a popular choice among our patrons, and the increased revenue was a welcome bonus.

I also made a point of getting to know each of the *exoleti* on a personal level, making sure they were comfortable with their work and addressing any concerns they might have. This included ensuring fair treatment and making certain they received adequate rest between clients. In turn, their newfound trust in me and increased morale translated into better experiences for the customers, who began to frequent our establishment more often.

"Ah, Io!" Salvius greeted me warmly as I entered his study, where he sat surrounded by scrolls and artifacts. "I must say, you've done wonders for Homo Domus."

"Thank you, Salvius," I replied, feeling a swell of pride at his praise. "I'm just glad I could help."

"Help? You've done more than help, my friend. Profits have never been higher, and the *exoleti* are happier than I've ever seen them," he said enthusiastically. "You've truly outdone yourself."

"Thank you, sir. I've tried to apply what I know about running a business to our unique... establishment," I explained, trying not to give away the fact that my knowledge came from a time two millennia in the future.

"Whatever your methods, they're working. I've decided to reward you with a bonus for your efforts," Salvius said, retrieving a small pouch of coins from his desk and handing it to me.

"Thank you, Salvius. That's very generous of you," I replied, gratefully accepting the pouch. The weight of the coins felt reassuring in my hand, a tangible symbol of my success in this foreign world.

"Generosity is easy when one is prosperous, Io. Keep up the good work, and there may be more where that came from," he said with a wink.

"Of course, sir. Thank you again."

As I left Salvius's study, my thoughts turned towards my new life in Pompeii. While running a brothel wasn't exactly what I'd had in mind when I first arrived in this ancient city, I found myself enjoying the challenges it presented. And as I walked through the halls of Homo Domus, listening to the laughter and satisfied sighs of both the *exoleti* and their clients, I knew that my efforts were making a difference—and that was worth more to me than any amount of coins.

* * *

The warm water of the baths washed over me, soothing my tired muscles after a long day's work. I leaned back against the edge of the pool, enjoying the quiet of the room. It was a rare moment of peace in the bustling brothel.

"Ah, Io," Salvius said as he entered the room and slipped into the water beside me. "I see you've discovered one of the finer perks of your new position."

"Indeed," I replied with a smile. "A well-earned respite, if I do say so myself."

"Speaking of which," he continued, "I wanted to congratulate you on your continued success here at Homo Domus. You've truly turned this place around."

"Thank you, Salvius. I couldn't have done it without the support of everyone here."

He nodded in agreement. "Our little family has come to trust you implicitly, Io. They know that you have their best interests at heart, and it shows in their performance."

As we soaked in silence for a moment, I found myself contemplating the future. With each passing day, the impending eruption of Mount Vesuvius weighed more heavily on my mind. I knew what lay ahead, but how could I save these people without revealing the truth about myself? No one would believe that I had come from the future—not even Salvius, who trusted me completely.

"Salvius," I began tentatively, "have you ever considered the possibility that something terrible might befall Pompeii?"

He raised an eyebrow, clearly puzzled by the question. "What do you mean?"

"Like a natural disaster, or... something worse."

"Ah, I see," he said, nodding thoughtfully. "Well, the gods can be capricious, as we all know. But I've never known them to unleash their wrath without cause. We live good lives here, Io. We treat others with respect and honor the gods in our actions. I find it hard to believe that they would arbitrarily destroy our city."

"Of course," I agreed, trying to hide my disappointment. It was clear that even Salvius—who had come to trust me so completely—would not entertain the idea of an impending catastrophe without concrete evidence.

"Besides," he continued with a grin, "the odds of such a thing happening during our lifetimes are colossally low. I'd say we're safer here than anywhere else in the empire."

I forced a smile, but inwardly I cringed at his words. If only he knew how wrong he was.

"By the way, Io," Salvius said, changing the subject, "I've been meaning to ask you about your background. We know so little about you, and yet you've managed to become such an important part of our lives."

"I come from a land far away called Minnesota. I said, resorting to the truth once more. "I doubt you've even heard of it. It's so far that I fear I may never find my way back. Then again, your kindness and hospitality has been such that I could make Pompeii my home."

"You would be a welcome neighbor. I have come to value your friendship. So how did your travels lead you here?

"Ah, well, that's a long story," I replied evasively. The truth was far too unbelievable, even for someone as open-minded as Salvius.

"Perhaps one day you'll share it with us," he said gently. "But for now, let us enjoy this moment of tranquility together, my friend."

"Indeed," I agreed, forcing the thought of Pompeii's doom from my mind for the time being. As the warm water enveloped me and Salvius's steady presence calmed my nerves, I allowed myself to forget, if only for a little while, the terrible burden of knowledge that I carried.

* * *

I couldn't shake the feeling of impending doom that hung over my heart like a dark cloud. Despite the beauty and tranquility of Pompeii, I knew its days were numbered. Climbing to the top of Vesuvius felt like a necessary pilgrimage, as if by confronting the mountain, I could somehow come to terms with the fate of this city I'd come to love. As I stood at the peak of the volcano, I gazed up at the night sky, marveling at its beauty. The absence of light pollution allowed the stars to shine in all their glory, casting an ethereal glow on the landscape below. It was breathtaking, and for a moment, I forgot the terrible secret I carried.

It was a different sky from the one I remembered. Stars drift as the universe expands. Some of them weren't even there anymore in my time. Now and then a meteor would streak across the sky. I'd have made a wish but I knew it was futile.

"Damn you," I whispered to the mountain, my voice full of sorrow and anger. "Why must you bring such destruction upon these people who have done nothing to deserve it?"

The mountain, of course, offered no reply—but in my mind, I imagined it smirking back at me, its silence taunting me.

"Perhaps I can save them," I mused, though I knew how impossible that task would be. "If only there were a way to make them believe..."

"Believe what?" a voice asked from behind me.

Startled, I turned to see Marcus standing there, his handsome face illuminated by the starlight. He must have followed me up here without my noticing.

"Ah, Marcus," I said, trying to regain my composure. "I didn't hear you approach."

"Didn't mean to sneak up on you," he replied with a warm smile. "What were you saying about making people believe something?"

"Nothing important," I lied, not wanting to burden him with my secret. Instead, I gestured toward the heavens. "Have you ever seen anything so beautiful?"

"Never," he admitted, joining me in gazing at the sky.

"Let me show you something," I said, eager to share the knowledge of my time with him. I pointed out each of the major stars—Betelgeuse, Polaris, Rigel, Sirius—and told him the myths and legends surrounding them. I also showed him the planets Mercury, Venus, Mars, Jupiter, and Saturn, explaining that they were not stars at all, but worlds like our own, orbiting the same sun we did.

"Other planets have moons, just like our Earth has its Luna," I continued, swept up in the excitement of sharing this information. "And it's quite possible that other stars have planets as well—perhaps even with life on them."

Marcus's eyes widened with fascination, even if he didn't fully understand the concepts I was describing. "I never knew any of this," he admitted. "You have such incredible knowledge, Io. Where did you learn all this?"

As we stood there, high atop Vesuvius, I couldn't forget the mountain's dark secret. Yet for one fleeting moment, under the canopy of stars, the world seemed full of endless possibilities, and I wished with all my heart that Marcus and I could explore them together—far away from the shadow of destruction that loomed over Pompeii.

The stars shimmered above us like a tapestry of diamonds, their brilliance enhanced by the inky blackness that enveloped the night. Marcus and I stood there, side by side, our hands entwined as we gazed at the celestial panorama before us. The cool mountain breeze danced around us, bringing with it the faint scent of the sea.

"Look, Io," Marcus whispered, his voice barely audible over the wind. "It's like the gods themselves are watching over us."

"Perhaps they are," I agreed, my heart swelling with emotion. I couldn't help but be awed by the beauty of this moment—the connection between us amplified by the serenity of our surroundings. And yet, I was painfully aware of how fleeting it all was.

"Marcus," I began, feeling an urgency rise within me. "I want to share something special with you, here and now, under the stars."

His dark brown eyes met mine, curiosity and warmth mingling within them. "What do you have in mind?"

"Something intimate, something that transcends both time and space," I said, my voice unsteady. "Let us make love right here, atop this mountain, and let the heavens bear witness to our passion."

Marcus looked at me intently for a moment, then smiled gently. "I can think of nothing more perfect," he agreed, leaning in to kiss me tenderly.

Our lips met, and the world seemed to fall away. Every touch, every caress felt heightened, imbued with the raw power of nature that surrounded us. We undressed each other slowly, deliberately, as if we had all the time in the world.

"Did you know," I murmured into Marcus's ear as I let my fingers trace patterns on his skin, "that the ancient Egyptians believed that when two people made love, their souls became intertwined?"

"Is that so?" Marcus replied, his breath hitching as I continued my exploration of his body. "Then let our souls entwine, Io."

We moved together as one, each movement a dance of love and desire. The stars above seemed to grow brighter with each passing moment, casting their ethereal glow upon our united forms.

"Marcus," I whispered, the name like a prayer on my lips, "no matter what happens in the future, this moment—here, with you—will forever be etched in my heart."

"Mine too, Io," he replied, his voice thick with emotion. "For all eternity."

As we reached the apex of our passion, it felt as if the universe itself was celebrating our love, the starlight bathing us in its celestial embrace. If only for that brief moment, we were infinite, and nothing could tear us apart.

As we lay there afterward, wrapped in each other's arms and gazing up at the sky, I couldn't help but wonder what fate had in store for us. Would we somehow manage to escape the impending doom that loomed over Pompeii? Or were we destined to become yet another tragic tale, lost to the sands of time?

"Marcus," I said quietly, my voice barely audible over the sound of our breathing, "Promise me one thing."

"Anything," he murmured, his eyes reflecting the constellations above us.

"Promise me that no matter what happens, our love will never fade—that it will shine just as brightly as these very stars."

"Even if the heavens themselves should fall," Marcus vowed, his grip tightening around me, "our love will endure."

And so, under the watchful gaze of the gods, we sealed our bond, our love transcending both time and space, forever reaching for the stars.

CHAPTER XI

The sun dipped low in the sky, painting the horizon in hues of orange and pink as I led Quintus to the abandoned temple. He seemed tense, his hands clenched into fists at his sides while his jaw set with determination. I knew full well how much Felix meant to him, but I couldn't help but feel a sense of disdain for these Followers and their beliefs. Yet, if it gave Quintus even an inkling of hope, I would swallow my pride and play along.

"Quintus," I said, placing a hand on his shoulder, "are you certain you want to do this?" I gazed into his eyes, searching for any hint of doubt.

He took a deep breath, then nodded. "Yes, Io. I must try one last time to win Felix back."

"Very well," I replied, reassuringly squeezing his shoulder. "Just remember, let me do the talking. I know enough about their beliefs to fool them."

As we approached the entrance of the temple, the dilapidated structure loomed above us, its once-grand facade now crumbling and overgrown with vines. The irony was not lost on me; a place that once worshipped the old gods now served as a meeting spot for this new religion.

"Alright," I whispered, stepping forward into the temple's dusty remains, "just follow my lead." Quintus nodded, his face etched with worry.

The interior of the temple was dimly lit by flickering torches, casting eerie shadows on the walls as they danced in the drafty air.

Huddled in the center were the Followers, their faces solemn and subdued, like sheep waiting for their shepherd.

"Peace be with you, brothers and sisters," I called out, feigning a warmth I did not feel.

They turned toward us, their gazes filled with suspicion. I braced myself, ready to defend my knowledge of their scriptures against any doubt they might have.

"Who are you?" one of them asked, her voice wavering with uncertainty.

"I am Iosephus," I replied, "and this is Quintus. We've come seeking fellowship and understanding."

"Iosephus?" a familiar voice called out from the shadows. Felix stepped forward, his eyes locking onto Quintus with a mixture of surprise and pain. "The false profit who has been fear-mongering throughout the city? And Quintus, the sodomite?"

"Hello, Felix," Quintus muttered, his voice barely audible.

"Enough!" I interjected, drawing their attention back to me. "We are here in peace. Let us not dwell on the past, but instead find solace in the teachings of the One."

"Very well," the woman said, seemingly appeased by my words. "Join us, then."

As we integrated ourselves into the gathering, I couldn't help but feel a strange sense of satisfaction. Perhaps I could use my knowledge to heal the rift between Quintus and Felix—or, at the very least, give Quintus the closure he so desperately needed. And if it meant pulling the wool over the eyes of these misguided Followers, then so be it.

A hulking figure blocked our path at the entrance to the abandoned temple, his sword glinting menacingly in the dim light. Caius, Ovidius's second in command, was not known for his intellect, and judging by the suspicious glare he leveled at us, I knew my wits would have to be sharp to gain entry.

"Who are you and what do you want?" he growled, his grip tightening on the sword's hilt.

"Peace, brother," I said confidently, drawing a sword of my own. In the dirt floor, I used its tip to trace a curved line. "We come seeking fellowship."

Caius studied the line for a moment, then cautiously added a second curve, forming the icthus—the secret symbol of the Followers. He lowered his weapon and stepped aside, granting us entry. My heart pounded in my chest, but I kept my face impassive, unwilling to betray my relief.

We were immediately confronted by Ovidius, the leader of the local Followers cell. His keen gaze swept over us, as if searching for any sign of deception. "You claim to be one of us," he said, addressing me directly. "Prove it."

"Ask me anything," I replied boldly, prepared to defend my knowledge of their scriptures. "I will show you that I am a true believer."

"Very well," Ovidius smirked. "Can you handle snakes? Drink poison? Cast out demons? Speak in tongues?"

My mind raced as I considered how best to respond. I had anticipated scriptural challenges, not these tests of faith. But I refused to be deterred. "Handling snakes and drinking poison can be mere tricks," I said, trying to downplay the importance of those signs. "As for casting out demons, I have performed exorcisms in His name. And speaking in tongues..." I hesitated, knowing that my knowledge of exotic languages might be seen as further evidence of my deceit.

"Go on," Ovidius urged, his eyes narrowing.

"Speaking in tongues is a gift from the Holy Spirit," I said, carefully choosing my words. "It is not something to be displayed to prove one's faith. It is a sacred communication with the divine." The room went quiet as I dropped to my knees, trembling. My heart raced as I prepared to put on a show for these Followers. I rolled my eyes back into my head and began reciting the Lord's Prayer in English, a language that didn't even exist. The words felt strange on my tongue, but they borrowed enough from Latin that I hoped the Followers would recognize them.

"Our Father who art in heaven, hallowed be thy name. Thy kingdom come, thy will be done on earth as it is in heaven. Give us this day our daily bread and forgive us our trespasses, as we forgive those who trespass against us," I intoned dramatically. The Followers exchanged glances, their faces filled with awe and confusion. Then, one by one, they began to join in, praying along in their native tongues. Their voices rose in unison, filling the air with the familiar cadence of the sacred words. I couldn't help but feel a thrill of victory; I had fooled them into thinking I was one of them.

Felix had thought of a way to get involved in my charade. His expression was tense, his eyes flicking between Felix and me. "I must testify," he announced, his voice shaking slightly. "It was Io who cast out my demons and cured me of my sinful lust."

Felix's eyes widened in disbelief, his gaze locked on Quintus. But before he could say anything, Ovidius interjected. "Is this true?" he asked, looking to me for confirmation.

"Indeed," I replied, trying to suppress the smirk that threatened to break across my face. "Through His power, I was able to free Quintus from the grip of temptation."

Ovidius studied me for a moment, then nodded in acceptance. "Praise be to the One for his mercy and power," he declared, raising his hands in a gesture of worship. The other Followers echoed his praise, their voices swelling with fervor.

But Felix remained silent, his eyes still locked on Quintus. The tension between them was palpable, and I could see the pain etched on both their faces. Felix looked betrayed and heartbroken while Quintus struggled to maintain a stoic facade.

As the meeting continued, I couldn't help but feel a twinge of guilt for my part in driving a wedge between the two former lovers. But I had come here to help Quintus, and if this was what he wanted, then so be it.

With a deep breath, I steadied myself as Ovidius began to read aloud from a scroll, his voice heavy with conviction. "Wherefore he also gave them up to uncleanness through the lusts of their own hearts, to dishonor their own bodies between themselves: Who changed the truth into a lie, and worshipped and served the creature more than the Creator, who is blessed forever."

As he continued, something about the words seemed familiar—too familiar. A memory flickered in my mind, and before I knew it, laughter bubbled up from within me, cutting Ovidius off mid-sentence.

"Those are not the words of the One!" I cried out in shock. "But I recognize them! I have heard them before." I exclaimed, still chuckling. The entire room fell silent, all eyes on me. I didn't care; I had to share this revelation. "I heard these very words spoken by none other than Saul of Tarsus when I saw him in a bar in Ephesus, bragging about killing a hundred Christians in one day!"

The atmosphere in the room shifted immediately. Caius's face paled, his eyes narrowing as he stared at me, anger and disbelief etched into his features. I could practically feel the hatred for Saul of Tarsus radiating off of him. Everyone knew that Saul had crucified his parents while Caius watched, helpless.

"Paulus is Saul?" Caius demanded, his voice shaking with rage. "You expect us to believe that?"

"Believe what you will," I replied, shrugging nonchalantly. "But those words came from the very mouth of Saul himself. I was there. I saw. In his drunken stupor he bragged to his men that he had a new idea to destroy the church for good: from within!"

"Then we have been deceived!" Caius declared, looking around the room, seeking support from his fellow Followers.

"Wait," Ovidius interjected, trying to regain control of the situation. "Let us not be hasty in our judgments. We must consider the possibility that our spirit leader Paulus has been misunderstood or misquoted."

I could see the internal struggle playing out on Caius's face as his loyalty to Ovidius warred with his hatred for Saul. I knew that my little revelation had the potential to tear this group apart, and while I felt a pang of guilt at the chaos I was causing, I couldn't deny the thrill it gave me.

"Ovidius, you know as well as I do that these words are not the Savior's teachings," I pressed, hoping to drive the wedge even deeper. "How can we follow someone who cannot discern truth from falsehood?"

"Enough!" Ovidius barked. His eyes darted between me and Caius, trying to determine how to handle the situation.

As the room teetered on the edge of hysteria, I couldn't help but feel a strange satisfaction in the chaos I had provoked. Whether it would ultimately benefit Quintus and his quest to win back Felix, or simply serve to expose the Followers' hypocrisy, only time would tell. But for now, I reveled in the power I held over these people—a power forged by knowledge and cunning, and wielded with ruthless precision.

"Brothers, let me tell you the story of Saul's conversion," Ovidius interjected, raising his voice to regain control of the room. "Saul was once a persecutor of our faith, but on the road to Damascus, he was struck blind by a vision of the Savior himself. Then, he was reborn as Paulus and became a champion of our cause."

"And you believe that? I heard him making up that story!" I laughed. "If you believe it, I have a bridge to sell you!"

Ovidius looked at me strangely. "Why would I want to buy a bridge?"

Caius's eyes narrowed, his fists clenching at his sides. "You knew!" he shrieked at Ovidius. "All this time, you knew Paulus was Saul? The same man who crucified my parents while I watched?"

"Paulus is not the same man, Caius," Ovidius pleaded. "He has been transformed by the grace of the Savior, just as we all have. We must learn to forgive, even when it seems impossible."

"I don't think this is what the Savior meant by turning the other cheek," I said.

"Forgive?" Caius spat, his voice shaking with rage. "You expect me to forgive the man who laughed in my face as my parents took their last breaths, nailed to a cross? How can you ask that of me, Ovidius?"

The tension in the room had reached a breaking point, and it seemed as though every breath held the potential to ignite an explosion.

"Enough!" Ovidius bellowed, trying to restore order. "We are here to worship and support one another, not to tear each other apart!"

But it was too late. Caius lunged at Ovidius, fists flying. The two men grappled and tumbled to the ground, their struggle setting off a chain reaction of violence throughout the room. Fists and curses filled the air as the Followers turned on one another, divided by the revelation of Paulus's true identity.

"Come on," I whispered urgently to Quintus, seizing the opportunity to escape the chaos. He nodded, grabbing Felix by the arm as we made our way toward the exit.

As I reached the doorway, I paused for a moment, taking in the scene before me. It was a far cry from the unified gathering of believers it had been just moments ago. My gaze met Ovidius's across the room, his eyes filled with anger and betrayal.

"Let's go," Quintus urged me, and I tore my eyes away from Ovidius, stepping out into the night.

As I locked eyes with Ovidius cross the room, a cold rage seemed to emanate from him, chilling me to the bone. The fury in his stare was palpable, and it was clear that he now saw me as an enemy, just as Chronos the Soothsayer did. In that moment, I realized I had made another formidable adversary.

"Curse you, interloper!" Ovidius snarled in my direction, his voice barely audible over the cacophony of shouts and scuffles behind him. "You think you've won? You will pay for your deceit!"

His words sent a shiver down my spine, but I refused to let him see my fear. Instead, I smirked, trying to appear as though I held all the cards. "My work is done here," I replied, my voice laced with a confidence I didn't entirely feel. I turned on my heel, leaving the crumbling unity of the Followers behind me, and stepped into the moonlit night.

* * *

As we navigated the dimly lit streets of Pompeii, our sandals crunching on the gravel underfoot, I couldn't help but feel a sense of satisfaction at having disrupted the gathering. Though my motives may have been selfish, I had exposed a truth that needed to be revealed—one that had shattered the blind faith of those who worshiped Paulus.

Quintus walked beside me, his brow furrowed in thought. Felix trailed behind us, his own expression a mix of confusion and anger. I could only imagine the turmoil he must be feeling, having his entire belief system shaken to its core.

"Are you alright?" I asked Quintus, my voice barely above a whisper. "You seem troubled."

He looked at me for a moment, then sighed. "I don't know, Io. Did we do the right thing? Was it worth tearing apart their faith just so I could try to win Felix back?"

I considered his words, feeling the weight of guilt settling on my shoulders. "Only time will tell, Quintus," I answered quietly. "But sometimes, the truth is more important than blind devotion."

We left the temple behind, stepping into the dimming light of day as the sun dipped low in the sky. The scent of freshly baked bread from a nearby bakery filled the air, blending with the aroma of roasting meats and fragrant spices. The hustle and bustle of Pompeii's streets surrounded us; shopkeepers hawking their wares, children chasing after each other in games, and donkeys laden with goods plodding along.

"Oi, Io! Quintus!" a familiar voice called out to us. I turned to see Nuntius, a friend I had made amongst the locals, rushing towards us with an *Acta Diurna* clutched in his hand. He was panting, beads of sweat glistening on his forehead.

"Have you heard the news?" he puffed, holding out the paper for us to see. "Emperor Vespasian is dead!"

Quintus took the paper, scanning the text quickly. "What? How can it be? And what does this mean for us?"

"Four months," Nuntius replied gravely. "That's how long we have until the new Emperor takes over. Word has it there's already tension among the ruling class."

"Four months," I repeated distantly, thinking of something completely different.

"By Jupiter!" Quintus muttered, "Your prophecy…."

"Just come with me," I said, taking his hand. "I must speak to your father—now."

CHAPTER XII

Four months had passed since the death of Vespasian, and my prophecy had taken root within tsneakhe hearts of many in Pompeii. The city was now split between those who placed their faith in me and those who remained loyal to Chronos, the town's ancient soothsayer. I could feel the tension gripping the entire town as I walked its streets, the whispers and stares following me like shadows.

"Have you heard?" a woman asked her neighbor in hushed tones as I passed by. "They say Io predicted Vespasian's death, and there's a terrible fate awaiting us all."

"*Falsum nuntium!*" a old man scoffed loudly, his disdain for me clear in his eyes. "It's just one of Chronos' enemies trying to undermine him. We mustn't lose faith in our soothsayer!"

As the day of my prophecy approached, violence began to break out across the city. Fistfights erupted in the marketplace, arguments turned vicious in the public baths, and even families were torn apart by their differing beliefs. I couldn't help but feel responsible for this chaos, even though I knew it wasn't my fault. After all, I hadn't chosen to be sent back in time, nor did I have any control over the volcano that threatened to destroy everything these people held dear.

"Io, we should leave," Marcus whispered urgently as we navigated through the increasingly hostile crowd. "I fear what might happen if you're recognized."

"Perhaps you're right," I sighed, my heart heavy with guilt. But as we turned to go, a voice rang out above the din.

"Look! It's Io, the false prophet!" a man sneered, pointing in our direction. "Come to gloat about your lies, have you?"

"Leave him alone, Gaius," another man interposed, stepping protectively in front of me. "Io speaks the truth, and Chronos is a relic of the past."

"Truth?" Gaius spat, his face contorted in rage. "The only truth here is that you've all been duped by an outsider!"

"Enough!" I cried, unable to bear any more violence in my name. "Please, let's not fight amongst ourselves. We must all stand together if we're to survive what's coming."

"Stand with you?" Gaius laughed bitterly. "I'd sooner throw myself into *Etna*'s fiery maw than ally with a charlatan like you!"

Before I could react, Gaius lunged towards me, fist raised to strike. Marcus moved to intercept him, but it was too late—the first blow had already connected with my jaw, sending shockwaves of pain through my skull. The crowd roared as the fight escalated, chaos reigning supreme as Pompeii's fragile peace shattered around us.

"Marcus, we need to get out of here," I gasped, struggling to remain on my feet amidst the brawl. Even as my vision blurred and blood trickled from my split lip, I knew one thing for certain: the day of reckoning was fast approaching, and there would be no escaping the wrath of the gods.

* * *

The sun had barely risen, casting a soft glow through the window of my small chamber. The previous day's chaos left me reeling, and I decided that hiding away in Salvius' home was the only way to avoid further confrontation. Marcus, loyal as ever, remained by my side.

"Are you sure this is wise?" Marcus asked, his brow furrowed with concern. "People will talk if you don't show your face."

"Let them," I sighed, rubbing at the bruise that still throbbed on my jaw. "I cannot risk causing more harm to the people I'm trying to save."

"Salvius believes you," he reassured me, his hand finding mine and giving it a gentle squeeze. "He's making preparations to leave Pompeii, as are many others."

"Good," I murmured, relief momentarily washing over me. It felt like a triumph, albeit a small one, amidst the turmoil that gripped the city. "They must make haste. The end could come any day now."

"Salvius has secured passage on a grain ship leaving from the port tomorrow," Marcus continued. "He's sending Petrus, Tiberius, and Antonius ahead to secure lodgings in Misenium."

"They'll be safe there," I nodded. Misenium was where Pliny the Younger would be watching and recording the event for posterity. "The rest of us will follow once everything is ready."

"Then I suppose we should make the most of our time here," I mused, my gaze wandering to the intricate frescoes that adorned the walls of my chamber. Images of Apollo and Daphne, their tragic love story forever immortalized in vibrant pigments, served as a stark reminder of the fleeting nature of life in Pompeii.

"Indeed," Marcus agreed, his voice tinged with sadness. "It's strange to think that we may never see this place again."

"Perhaps it's for the best," I replied, my thoughts straying to Chronos and the violent divide his persistent skepticism had caused. "The city can only heal if we move forward, and that means leaving the past behind."

"Speaking of which," Marcus said, a wry smile appearing on his face. "Salvius told me he's made arrangements for Fabius to cook one last extravagant meal for us tonight. A farewell feast, if you will."

"Fabius?" I smiled, recalling the talented chef and his ability to create culinary masterpieces from even the most mundane ingredients. "How fitting. The end of an era marked by one final indulgence."

"Exactly," Marcus grinned, his eyes sparkling with amusement.

"Now, let's see if we can find you something to wear that won't draw attention at the feast tonight."

"Very well," I agreed, a small chuckle escaping my lips. "But only because it's Fabius' cooking."

As we rummaged through the trunks of clothing Salvius had provided, I couldn't help but marvel at how far we'd come since that fateful day when I first arrived in Pompeii. Despite the fear and uncertainty that lay ahead, there was solace in knowing that I had managed to make a difference in the lives of those who trusted me.

"Here," Marcus said, triumphantly holding up a simple tunic and cloak. "This should do the trick."

"Perfect," I replied, taking the garments from him and beginning to change. As I did so, I caught a glimpse of myself in a polished bronze mirror and paused for a moment, studying my reflection.

"Who would have thought that I could cause so much trouble?" I wondered aloud, more to myself than to Marcus.

"Your words carry weight because they ring true," Marcus said softly, coming to stand beside me. "The people of Pompeii may be divided now, but in time, they'll come to see that you spoke from a place of love and concern for their well-being."

"Thank you, Marcus," I whispered, my voice thick with emotion. "Your unwavering support means more to me than you'll ever know."

"Likewise," he replied, his eyes meeting mine in the mirror's reflection. "Now, let's go enjoy our last moments in this magnificent city before we must face the future."

"Agreed," I said, determination surging through me as I donned the cloak and prepared to step out into the fading twilight. "After a meal like that, I need a walk."

* * *

We emerged from the safety of Salvius's home, and I couldn't help but feel a mix of apprehension and determination. As we walked through the streets of Pompeii, I noticed how the once vibrant city had become a battleground between those who believed in my prophecy and those who remained loyal to Chronos.

"Look!" Marcus whispered, pointing at a wall where someone had written in charcoal, "Io is a false prophet! Only Chronos speaks the truth!"

"Pay it no mind," I said, trying to hide my disappointment. But it was difficult to ignore the whispers and sideways glances as we passed by the citizens of Pompeii. Some even went so far as to throw rotten fruit at us as we hurried along.

"Over there," Marcus gestured to a crowd gathered around Chronos himself, who stood on an elevated platform, his boney hands clutching a staff adorned with the bones of small animals. "He's been denouncing you every day for the past week."

"Let's move closer," I said, pulling my hood over my head to remain inconspicuous.

"Friends, countrymen, listen closely!" Chronos cackled, his voice high-pitched and shrill. "Do not be deceived by this stranger who dares to challenge the wisdom of the gods! His prophecies are nothing more than lies meant to sow discord among us!"

"Chronos has never steered us wrong before!" shouted a man in the crowd. Others voiced their agreement, angrily condemning me for my perceived deception.

"Enough," I muttered under my breath, feeling anger and frustration coursing through my veins. "Let's go find Salvius. We've seen enough."

"Agreed," Marcus replied, his hand resting protectively on my shoulder as we turned away from the fervent mob.

As we approached Salvius's estate, we found him directing his servants and family members as they loaded carts with their belongings. He had decided to evacuate Pompeii as a precaution, trusting my prophecy enough to put his faith in me.

"Salvius!" I called out, waving at him from a distance.

"Ah, Io! Just the man I wanted to see," he replied, his face lighting up with relief. "I'm glad you're here. I've been making arrangements for my family and staff to leave the city. They'll travel ahead of us, and we'll rendezvous in Misenium."

"Are you sure about this?" I asked, unable to keep the worry from my voice.

"Undoubtedly. Your prophecy has shaken me to my core, and the rumblings beneath our feet only serve to confirm my suspicions. We must leave Pompeii before it's too late," Salvius said with determination.

"Then let us make haste," I urged, grateful for his unwavering faith in me. As his family and servants began their journey, I couldn't help but wonder if I was leading them all toward salvation or further into the abyss.

* * *

As we returned to Salvius' home, the scent of Fabius' cooking no longer lingered. The once bustling estate now lay quiet and empty, its inhabitants already on their way to safety. I couldn't shake the feeling that this might be my last visit here. A heavy realization settled in my chest as I glanced around the familiar surroundings.

"Marcus, there's something I need to do before we leave," I said, heading toward his chamber.

"What is it?" he asked, concern etched on his face.

"Call it a farewell message—perhaps a piece of history," I replied cryptically, not wanting to reveal too much about my origins. As I entered Marcus' room, I found a charcoal stick among the scattered belongings. With swift strokes, I scrawled a message on the wall.

Marcus looked at me quizzically but didn't question my actions. Instead, he simply shook his head. "I don't get it."

"That's okay," I answered with a cryptic smile. "Somebody will—someday."

A sudden commotion caught our attention as we walked out of the house. Chronos approached us with a group of *vigiles urbani*, the city watchmen, in tow. "Ah, Iosephus Andrius and Marcus Andronicus! Just the deviants I've been seeking!" Chronos sneered, his gaunt frame casting an eerie shadow over the cobblestone street. "You thought you could spread lies and chaos throughout

Pompeii without consequence? You have undermined the authority of the gods themselves!"

"Chronos, we're just trying to save lives," I pleaded, clutching Marcus' hand tightly.

"Enough!" Chronos barked, signaling the *vigiles urbani* to seize us. As they roughly grabbed our arms, I couldn't help but feel the weight of my decisions bearing down on me. Was this the price for meddling with the past and attempting to alter fate?

"Let us go!" Marcus shouted defiantly, struggling against their hold.

"Silence!" Chronos commanded, his voice like a whip. "By order of the city magistrate, you are both under arrest for inciting panic and disorder. You will be brought before the court to face judgment."

"Chronos, please listen to reason," I begged as the watchmen tightened their grip on us. "We don't have much time left!"

"Your lies will fall on deaf ears, Io," he spat at me, and with a cruel grin, he added, "Enjoy your last moments in Pompeii."

As we were forcefully led away by the *vigiles urbani*, I couldn't shake the feeling that time was running out—not just for Marcus and me, but for everyone who remained in Pompeii.

The cold iron shackles bit into my wrists as we were led through the streets of Pompeii. Marcus and I were paraded like criminals, our hands bound and heads hung low. The reason for our arrest? Inciting panic and disorder amongst the citizens of Pompeii with our warnings of the impending eruption of Vesuvius. In their eyes, we were dangerous heretics who threatened the stability of their world.

"Look at them!" sneered a woman to my left, clutching a clay amulet of Mars, the god of war, in her trembling hand. "They deserve everything that's coming to them."

"Traitors!" spat an old man, hobbling alongside us on his gnarled wooden cane.

"May the Furies torment you for your lies!" another voice bellowed from the crowd.

Marcus clenched his jaw, anger flaring in his eyes. He looked ready to snap, but I squeezed his hand tightly, urging him to keep his composure. Seeing the people we sought to save treating us with such contempt pained me, but I couldn't let it deter us from our mission. The fate of Pompeii was at stake.

"Stay strong, love," I whispered to Marcus, feeling the weight of his fear and frustration. "We'll find a way out of this mess."

"Io, I..." he began, his voice cracking with emotion. "I'm scared. What if we can't convince them? What if they don't listen?"

"Have faith, Marcus," I replied, trying to sound more confident than I felt. "We've come too far to give up now."

As we reached the doors of the city magistrate's court, my heart pounded in my chest like a legionary's drum. Time was slipping through my fingers like sand in an hourglass, and I knew that every second I spent in custody brought Pompeii closer to its doom.

"May Fortuna be with us," I murmured as the doors creaked open, and we stepped into the grand chamber to face our fate.

The jail cell where Marcus and I found ourselves was a dimly lit, dank chamber. The air smelled of decay and unwashed bodies, and the stone walls seemed to close in on us with every passing moment. A small, barred window high up on one wall allowed just enough light to seep in, casting eerie shadows across the floor. The iron bars that separated us from the outside world were cold and unyielding, a stark reminder of our current predicament.

A handful of other prisoners were in the cell with us, each staring at us with a mixture of curiosity and contempt. I could feel their eyes on me as Marcus and I settled onto the hard-packed dirt floor, trying to find some semblance of comfort amidst the filth and despair. We huddled together for warmth and support, knowing that we'd need to rely on each other if we were going to survive this ordeal.

"Oi, newcomers," called out a gruff voice from the far corner of the cell. A burly man with unkempt hair and a thick beard ambled toward us, followed by two others who appeared to be his cronies. "What are you in for?"

"Disturbing the peace," I replied cautiously, not wanting to reveal too much about my prophecy. "We... uh... got into an argument with some people in the market."

"Ha! That's nothing compared to what we've done," boasted the burly man, puffing out his chest with pride. "Me and my mates here are in for robbery and assault. We're real criminals!"

"Congratulations," Marcus muttered sarcastically under his breath. He was clearly unimpressed by our cellmates' bravado, but I nudged him in the ribs to remind him to be cautious. It wouldn't do us any good to make enemies in here.

"Anyway," the burly man continued, undeterred by Marcus' indifference, "the name's Gnaeus. These two are Decimus and Sextus. And you?"

"Io," I replied, offering a small smile despite my growing unease. "And this is Marcus."

"Io, huh?" Gnaeus snorted. "Never heard of that name before. You must be one of those foreigners from the far reaches of the empire. How'd you end up in Pompeii?"

"Long story," I said evasively, not wanting to share my true origin with these strangers. "What about you? Are you from here?"

"Born and raised," Gnaeus replied, chuckling darkly. "But I'll be damned if I die in this wretched place. If I ever get out of here, I'm going to start fresh somewhere else. Maybe Gaul or Hispania. Somewhere without so many bloody rules."

"Sounds like a plan," I agreed, trying to keep the conversation light. "We all deserve a second chance, right?"

"Damn straight," Gnaeus said, nodding enthusiastically. "Anyway, don't let this place get to you. We're all in the same boat here. Just stick together, and we'll make it through."

As Gnaeus and his friends wandered back to their corner of the cell, I couldn't help but think about how misguided their aspirations were. They wanted to escape Pompeii because of its rules, while I fought desperately to save the city from a fate far worse than any jail cell.

"Io," Marcus whispered, his voice trembling with fear, "what are we going to do? We can't stay here. The people need us. Pompeii needs us."

"I know, love," I murmured, holding him close. "But we have to bide our time. There must be a way out of here, and when we find it, we'll do everything in our power to save our city. I promise."

"May the gods help us," Marcus whispered, his eyes filled with tears. "For if they don't, who will?"

* * *

The darkness of the night enveloped Pompeii, its inky fingers reaching into every corner and alleyway. From my spot on the cold stone floor of the jail cell, I watched as the last rays of sunlight disappeared behind the horizon, leaving us to face the unknown that awaited in the shadows. The quiet was unnerving—starkly contrasting to the bustling city beyond these walls. "Io," Marcus whispered so softly I could barely hear him above the distant murmurs of the other prisoners. "Do you think they'll come for us?"

"Who?" I asked, not quite following his train of thought.

"Salvius... or our friends. Do you think they know we're here?"

"I hope so," I replied, trying to sound confident despite the gnawing uncertainty in my gut. As much as I wanted to believe someone would rescue us from this nightmare, I couldn't ignore the real possibility that we were alone. Our fate rested entirely in our hands, and that reality weighed heavily upon me.

"Oi! You two lovebirds!" a gruff voice called out from across the cell. I turned to see a burly man with a tangled mass of hair and an unkempt beard approaching us. "You've been whispering sweet nothings to each other all day. Why don't you share some of that affection with the rest of us, eh?"

"Leave them alone, Calvus," another prisoner interjected. "They're not bothering anyone."

"Mind your own business, Aulus," Calvus shot back. "I'm just having a bit of fun with the new boys."

"Fun," I muttered under my breath, rolling my eyes. I knew we needed allies, not enemies, but it was difficult to remain calm when faced with such blatant cruelty. Their laughter died away as the cell shook, dust falling down from the ceiling.

"Did you hear that?" I whispered urgently to Marcus, who had also been startled by the noise.

"Thunder?" he asked, his voice trembling slightly.

"Perhaps," I said hesitantly, though deep down, I knew this was no ordinary storm. The gods were speaking, and their message was clear: time was running out.

CHAPTER XIII

23 October 79 C.E.

I stood there, bound and helpless, with Marcus beside me. His hands trembled slightly, but he managed to keep his composure as we were brought before Septimus Caerellius, Pompeii's stern-faced magistrate. The room was filled with the scent of incense, offering a thin veil against the mounting tension in the air. The sound of my racing heart seemed to echo off the stone walls.

"State your names," Septimus ordered, his voice booming through the hall.

"Iosephus Andrius," I replied, trying to keep my voice steady.

"Marcus Andronicus," Marcus said, his voice cracking slightly.

"Very well," Septimus continued, his eyes narrowing at us. "Iosephus, you stand accused of causing widespread panic among the people of Pompeii with your dire warnings. Marcus Antonius, you are accused of being an accomplice to these actions. How do you plead?"

"Your Honor," I began, searching for the right words, "We did not intend to cause panic. We sought only to warn our fellow citizens of an impending disaster."

A tremor rumbled beneath us as if on cue, shaking the floor and rattling the ornate vases lining the walls. I saw fear flicker in Septimus' eyes for just a moment before he regained control and attempted to ignore the quake.

"Enough!" he snapped, dismissing the tremor as mere coincidence. "I will not have my courtroom disrupted by unfounded claims or wild tales. You will present evidence to support your allegations, or you will face the consequences of your actions."

"Your Honor, I assure you our warnings are not without merit," I tried to explain, careful not to reveal my true origins. "My knowledge comes from reliable sources, ones that I cannot disclose here. But I beg you to consider that these tremors may be a sign of things to come."

"Silence!" Septimus roared, slamming his gavel against the wooden podium. The sound echoed through the chamber like a thunderclap. "I will not entertain such foolish notions. Your fate rests in the hands of the evidence provided and the testimonies given."

"Please, Your Honor," Marcus pleaded, desperation evident in his voice. "We meant no harm. We only wanted to protect our friends and neighbors from potential danger."

"Your misguided attempts have led to chaos and fear," Septimus chastised, his expression darkening. "If you cannot provide substantial evidence or witnesses to support your claims, I have no choice but to render judgment."

Another tremor shook the room, this one more violent than the last. Dust fell from the ceiling, and the onlookers murmured anxiously amongst themselves. Septimus clenched his jaw and gripped the edge of the podium, his knuckles turning white.

"Order! Order in the court!" he bellowed, fighting to maintain control as the tremors subsided.

"Your Honor," I implored, seizing the opportunity, "These tremors are growing stronger, more frequent. Can't you see that they lend credence to our warnings?"

"Enough!" Septimus shouted, silencing me with a furious glare. "I will hear no more. Testimonies will be presented, and then I shall pass judgment."

I couldn't help but feel a sense of dread wash over me. It was becoming increasingly clear that the truth was not enough to sway Septimus' mind. My thoughts raced, searching for a way to save

Marcus and myself from an uncertain fate. Time was running out, and if I didn't act soon, we would both be lost to the sands of history. "Chronos the Soothsayer, please take the stand," Septimus announced, his voice echoing through the chamber.

The tall, thin man glided to the stand, his dark eyes fixed on me with a mixture of disdain and triumph. As the town augur, Chronos was highly respected among the citizens of Pompeii. His predictions were unnervingly accurate, and I knew his testimony would carry weight in this trial, even if it was tainted by rivalry.

"Your Honor," Chronos began, his voice dripping with contempt, "Iosephus is not only an outsider but a dangerous instigator. He has spread false rumors about the impending destruction of our beloved city, causing chaos and fear throughout our streets."

I clenched my fists, feeling the hot anger rise within me. How could he be so blind to the reality that was about to befall us all?

"Your accusations are baseless," I retorted. "All I've tried to do is warn people of what I know is coming."

"Silence!" Septimus commanded, cutting off my protest. "You will have your chance to speak, Iosephus. Let Chronos finish his testimony."

"Thank you, Your Honor," Chronos said smugly, taking advantage of my outburst. "Not only has this man caused unnecessary panic, but he has also dared to challenge my authority as the town's trusted soothsayer. He claims to have knowledge of events that not even the gods themselves could predict."

"Very well," Septimus interrupted, nodding for Chronos to step down. "Ovidius Aurius, please come forward."

A hulking figure approached the stand, his chiseled features twisted into a scowl. Ovidius bore a particular hatred for me. I braced myself for whatever falsehoods he would conjure against me. "Your Honor," he began, his voice a low growl, "this man is more than just a troublemaker. He is a sorcerer who used black magic to kill Vespasian, our former leader and a devoted servant of the gods."

My heart sank as I realized the gravity of this accusation. To be accused of sorcery and murder was a death sentence in Pompeii.

I had to think fast, find some way to discredit their testimonies without revealing my true origins.

"Sorcery?" I laughed. "How much wine have you had to drink today?"

"I do not drink wine."

"Really? Why not?"

"I just don't like it." Ovidius said. "How is it that you knew when Vespasian would die?"

"I never said I knew when. Only that it would be the first sign, and that four months later—which is tomorrow—the prophecy will be fulfilled. And thanks to your wasting Septimus' time with these ridiculous proceedings, there will be no survivors."

"Did you hear that, Septimus?" Chronos shouted. "He just threatened Pompeii." He stared coldly at me. "How do we know that your prophecy did not cause Vespasian to die?"

"That was no prophecy, but a statement of fact. You will die too, Chronos... and you, Septimus... even I will die... someday. Everybody dies, Chronos. It does not take a seer to know that."

"Silence!" Septimus roared once again, his patience wearing thin. "You will have your chance to speak, Iosephus, but not now. Let Ovidius finish."

"Thank you, Your Honor," Ovidius sneered, clearly enjoying my distress. "This sorcerer infiltrated my family and tore us apart from within. He has disrupted the sacred balance of our city, and I fear his dark influence will only bring further ruin if left unchecked."

I turned back to Ovidius. "Who are you to accuse me? You, a heathen!" Shocked whispers went through the court. "Is it not true, Ovidius Aurius, that you are a member of the outlaw cult that was driven out of Pompeii? Not only a member, but their leader!"

"Irrelevant!" Chronos roared.

"Irrelevant? That the witness is an enemy of the empire, a disciple of the Nazarene?"

Shocked whispers went through the gallery. Ovidius was starting to sweat "No... no..."

"Do you deny it?"

"I... I..."

"A question has been asked, Ovidius. Answer it! Are you a follower of the Nazarene? Are you a Christian?"

"No! These are lies, your honor!"

"Then you reject the Nazarene? You deny him?"

"Yes," Ovidius whimpered in a small, quiet voice, a tear streaming down his cheek.

"Speak up!" I screamed at him. "The court must hear your voice. Now answer, before the gods and on your honor, do you reject the lies of the Nazarene?"

"Yes!" Ovidius screamed. *"I don't know the Nazarene you speak of!"*

I looked at Ovidius and smiled. Then I crowed like a rooster. Ovidius burst into tears.

Gotcha!

A small, shocked voice cried out from the back of the room. *"Mendax!"* I turned to see Felix standing there, tears streaming down his face. "Where is your faith now, Ovidius?"

"Felix!" Septimus gasped. "What are you doing here!"

"I had to see for myself," Felix said, coming forward to stare at Ovidius while he wept bitterly. "You lied to me. You lied to us all."

"What are you talking about?" Septimus demanded.

"What, you didn't know?" I asked the magistrate. "How could you not know that your own son was a... a Follower!"

A shocked hush went through the room. Septimus gaveled them to silence. A sudden tremor rippled through the floor, causing the walls to shudder and threatening to topple the oil lamps that lined them. Dust rained down from the ceiling as the shaking intensified, leaving an acrid taste in my mouth. Septimus paused mid-sentence, his eyes darting around the room with unease, but he quickly regained his composure.

"Proceed," he commanded, though his voice wavered ever so slightly.

"Your Honor," I called out, seizing the opportunity. "Do you not see? These tremors are a sign! They prove that my warnings were true!"

Septimus' steely gaze fell upon me. "Iosephus, do not try my patience. We are here to determine your actions' truth, not entertain your wild claims."

"Your Honor, please!" Salvius suddenly spoke up, standing beside me. "I have known Iosephus for some time now, and I can assure you that he is no sorcerer or murderer. He has been nothing but a good friend to me and others in this city."

"Silence!" The magistrate's gavel pounded against the table, echoing throughout the room like the crack of a whip. "You are here to testify, Marcellus, not to plead for leniency. You will have your chance to speak, but for now, sit down!"

"Your Honor, I must insist that you consider the possibility that Iosephus may be telling the truth." Salvius' voice was firm, yet laced with concern. "His intentions have always been pure, and I believe that he only wants what is best for Pompeii and its people."

As Salvius continued to argue on my behalf, I couldn't help but notice the furtive glances exchanged between Chronos and Ovidius. They wanted nothing more than to see me fail, their hatred for me fueled by their own insecurities and petty grievances. I knew that I had to find a way to turn the tide in my favor, to make Septimus see through their lies.

"Your Honor," I said, trying to keep my voice steady, "consider the tremors that have been plaguing our city these past few days. They have only grown stronger and more frequent, just as I predicted. Surely, this cannot be mere coincidence."

Septimus looked at me with an expression that was both skeptical and intrigued. "And what do you propose we do with this information, Iosephus?" he asked, his tone measured but not dismissive.

"Evacuate the city!" I implored, desperation coloring my words. "There is still time to save lives! Please, listen to reason!"

"Enough!" The gavel struck again, drowning out the murmurs that had begun to rise among the spectators. "I have heard enough. Salvius Marcellus, thank you for your testimony. You may be seated."

"Your Honor, please—" Salvius began, but was quickly silenced by another sharp rap of the gavel.

"Silence!" Septimus' face was now flushed with anger. "I will not allow this courtroom to devolve into chaos. We are here to uphold the law and ensure justice is served, not to entertain wild fantasies and baseless claims."

As Salvius reluctantly sat down, I knew that it would take more than his heartfelt plea to sway the magistrate in our favor. I could only hope that the truth would be enough to save us from the fate that seemed all but inevitable.

"Your Honor," I began, my voice wavering as I took the stand. "I stand before you not as a sorcerer or a madman, but as a man who has seen what is to come and wishes only to save lives." The tremors had subsided for the moment, but I could feel the tension in the air, like the calm before a storm.

"Throughout this trial," I continued, trying to steady my breath, "we have experienced these tremors, which serve as evidence of my claims. I cannot explain how I know what will happen, but I assure you that my intentions are pure."

As I spoke, I glanced over at Marcus, chained at the wrists and ankles, his eyes filled with fear. I knew I had to clear his name, even if it meant sealing my own fate. "Marcus Andronicus has done nothing wrong. He was merely an unwitting participant in my attempts to warn the people of Pompeii. Let it be me if anyone is to be punished, but spare him."

Septimus raised an eyebrow, clearly considering my words, when suddenly Ovidius stood up from his seat among the spectators, his face contorted into a sneer. "Your Honor," he bellowed, drawing all eyes to him, "this... this charlatan cannot be trusted! He has corrupted our city, spreading lies and chaos, and now he seeks to protect his accomplice... his lover!" His voice dripped with disdain as he spat out the last word.

"Enough, Ovidius!" Septimus snapped, his patience wearing thin. "I will decide who is guilty and who is innocent. You may sit down." Ovidius shot me a venomous look before reluctantly taking his seat.

"Your Honor," I implored once more, focusing on the magistrate. "I ask not for mercy, but for understanding. I only wanted to save lives. I beg you, please consider the evidence before you." I could feel the weight of the glances from the people around me, their whispers like invisible daggers.

"Save lives?" Septimus mused, looking thoughtful as he stroked his chin. "It is a noble sentiment, Iosephus, and one that I cannot easily dismiss. However, we must uphold the law."

My heart sank as I realized that my words had not swayed him, but I held onto a shred of hope that perhaps Marcus might still be spared. I turned my gaze again to my lover, silently promising that I would do everything in my power to set things right.

"Your Honor," Salvius interjected. "I have known Iosephus for a short time, but I can attest to his good character. He cares deeply for the people of Pompeii, and he would never wish harm upon them."

"Your words are heartfelt, Salvius," Septimus replied, unmoved. "However, the law must be upheld. Justice cannot yield to sentimentality."

As the magistrate spoke, I couldn't help but notice the cacophony of the bustling courtroom. The sound of the gavel striking the wooden block resonated like thunder, echoing off the stone walls that surrounded us. The burning incense wafted through the air, its sweet aroma mingling with the underlying stench of sweat and fear.

"Septimus," Salvius pleaded, desperation evident in his voice. "Please reconsider. Surely there must be another way."

"Enough!" Septimus roared, his frustration boiling over. "The evidence has been presented, and the testimonies heard. It is time for a verdict." His eyes swept over the crowd, daring anyone else to challenge him.

"Your Honor," I whispered, the weight of despair pressing down on me. "Please, just spare Marcus. He's innocent. He was only trying to help."

"Silence," Septimus commanded, his gaze piercing me like a dagger. "My decision is final."

My heart raced as the pounding of the gavel marked the end of our trial. The tremors beneath our feet seemed to intensify, yet everyone remained steadfast in their denial. In that moment, I knew that no matter how much I pleaded or fought, I could not change a man's mind so entrenched in his convictions.

Septimus leaned forward, his eyes narrowing as he announced our fate. "Iosephus and Marcus, you have been found guilty of causing panic and chaos in Pompeii. As such, I sentence you to be taken to Mons Mortis in the morning, where you will both be crucified. May the gods show you mercy."

My breath caught in my chest as the words sank in, Marcus' grip on my hand tightening painfully. The incense that filled the air, once a comforting reminder of home, now felt stifling, choking me as the reality of our situation set in.

"Your Honor," I tried one last time, desperation creeping into my voice. "Please, reconsider. We did not mean to cause harm; we were only trying to help."

"Enough!" Septimus slammed his gavel down, the sound echoing throughout the room like thunder. "You had your chance to defend yourselves, and it was not enough. Justice will be served."

I glanced over at Chronos, who stood smirking in the shadows, clearly pleased with the verdict. His gaze met mine, and for a moment, I saw a glimmer of satisfaction in those cold, calculating eyes. It sickened me to know that someone so influential in the community could take pleasure in another's pain.

Ovidius, on the other hand, appeared indifferent to our fate. He lazily toyed with the fringe of his robe, seemingly lost in thought. It baffled me how someone so powerful, someone who had once held sway over a group of followers, could simply not care about what happened to two men he had known, even if only briefly.

"Take them away!" Septimus ordered, his voice cold and unyielding.

As the guards grabbed hold of Marcus and me, dragging us from the courtroom, I couldn't help but think of our impending fate and the disaster that loomed over Pompeii. But even in the face of hopelessness, the burning desire to save Marcus and our doomed city remained.

"Marcus," I whispered as we were led down a dimly lit corridor. "Don't worry, I have a plan. We just need to time it perfectly."

"Io," he replied, his eyes filled with fear and trust. "I believe in you."

As we were led down the narrow corridor, torches casting flickering shadows on the walls, I racked my brain for any obscure historical facts about Roman prisons or Pompeii that might help our escape. The tremors continued to shake the ground beneath our feet, a constant reminder that time was running out.

* * *

The cold iron bars of the cell slammed shut, sending a shiver down my spine. The dimly lit jail was damp and smelled of mold and unwashed bodies. Marcus and I were thrown onto the dirty straw that covered the uneven stone floor. The sound of our harsh breathing filled the small space.

"Io," Marcus said, his voice trembling. "I'm scared."

I squeezed his hand reassuringly and forced a smile. "Don't worry, my love. I have a plan."

"Really?" His eyes searched mine, desperate for some sliver of hope.

"Really," I confirmed. "But we'll need to time it perfectly."

Marcus nodded, his faith in me evident in the face of such dire circumstances. As we lay there on the filthy floor, our bodies pressed together for warmth and comfort, I couldn't help but marvel at the strength of our love. It had sustained us through so much; now it would see us through this.

"Get some rest," I murmured into his hair. "We'll need our energy."

With that, Marcus closed his eyes and drifted off to a fitful sleep, his chest rising and falling with each shallow breath. I stayed awake, my mind racing as I plotted our escape. The tremors continued to rumble beneath us, a constant reminder that time was running out.

But I refused to let that deter me. For Marcus, for us, I would find a way. And I would do whatever it took to save the man I loved from the cruel fate that awaited us both on Mons Mortis.

CHAPTER XIV

It was the twenty-fourth of October. Volcano day had arrived. The sun was climbing higher in the sky as we made our way up the slope of Mons Mortis, a hill that loomed over Pompeii like a dark harbinger. This was the place where criminals met their end, and today it would be Marcus and I who were to join the ranks of the damned.

The hill's ground was stained with the blood of those crucified before us, patches of crimson seeping into the earth like gruesome flowers that bloomed on this forsaken land. I knew from my studies that death by crucifixion was particularly agonizing, with victims sometimes taking days to expire. A shudder ran through me at the thought—all my knowledge of history had never prepared me for being a part of it.

"Look at him," one of the vigiles sneered, pointing at me. "He's shaking like a leaf."

"Wouldn't you be?" another guard retorted, chuckling darkly. "He's about to meet Jupiter himself."

My mind raced as I tried to figure out how much time had passed since we left the city. With only the sun as my guide, I guessed it to be around 9:45 in the morning. Time was running out—or rather, it hurtled towards us like an unstoppable force, and I could do nothing to halt its advance. Faced with a tidal wave, there was only one thing I could do. I was going to have to surf.

"Enough chatter," a third guard barked, pushing us forward. "Let's get this over with."

A hushed murmur of anticipation rippled through the crowd that had gathered to witness our execution. Faces both familiar and strange stared back at us, their expressions a mixture of curiosity, fear, and morbid fascination. Among them were Chronos the soothsayer and Ovidius Aurius, their eyes gleaming with undisguised glee as they jeered at Marcus and me.

"Finally, we'll be rid of this bothersome foreigner!" Chronos cackled, his skeletal frame trembling with excitement.

"May Saturn himself strike you down, Iosephus!" Ovidius spat, shaking his fist in my direction.

But amidst the sea of hostility, there were also those who had come to show their support. Salvius Marcellus, the wealthy proprietor of Homo Domus, stood with his family, his face etched with concern. Petrus, Tiberius, and Antonius, the loyal *exoleti* from his brothel, also looked on with sorrowful eyes.

"Strength, Iosephus," Salvius whispered, offering me a small nod of encouragement.

"Silence!" one of the vigiles barked, raising his hand. "The condemned shall speak."

I swallowed hard, feeling a lump rise in my throat, and glanced at Marcus. Our eyes met for a brief moment, and in them, I saw an ocean of love and understanding. With a deep breath, I began to speak.

"O citizens of Pompeii, I stand before you today filled with regret that I could not save your great city. I have tried to protect you, but now I find myself powerless to do so."

Tears welled up in my eyes as I turned to Marcus. "And to you, Marcus Andronicus, my love, my heart, know that I gladly face death, knowing that we shall die together. For eternity shall not separate us."

I paused, taking a deep breath, and then continued. I had to stall for time for as long as I could, mere minutes by my reckoning. Right now, time was the only friend I had left. "Heed my words, people of Pompeii: the Roman Empire will fall. Emperors shall rise and fall—Hadrian, who will build his great wall; Constantine, who will unite the empire under one faith; Marcus Aurelius, the philosopher king who will lead Rome through its twilight years."

"Madness!" Chronos shouted, but I ignored him and pressed on.

"Beyond Rome, other empires shall rise and fall, both good and evil. Someday men will walk upon the moon—the orb you believe to be Diana's chariot."

The crowd gasped, unsure whether to believe or dismiss my words as the ravings of a madman. But I knew I needed to stall for time, waiting for Vulcan to intervene.

A rumbling of thunder began to rise as I moved in for the big finish. "Indeed, I know these things because..." I hesitated for a moment, locking eyes with Marcus, who nodded encouragingly. "I am from the future!" The crowd erupted into whispers of disbelief and astonishment.

"Preposterous!" Chronos sneered, his bony fingers trembling with rage. "You're nothing but a fraud!"

"These things all came to pass long before I was born!" I shouted above the cacophony of voices, my heart racing. "The gods have brought me back from the far future to put right what once went wrong!"

"Enough!" Ovidius roared, but I would not be silenced.

"Listen well, for it is not just empires that will change! The very way we live shall be transformed! Slavery will be abolished, diseases cured, and great machines will carry us across the land and skies!" I could see confusion and fear spreading through the crowd, unsure whether to mock or believe me.

"Silence him!" Chronos hissed to the vigiles, but the ground beneath our feet began to tremble before they could act. The rumbling rose to a deafening crescendo. Chronos swayed like a branch in the wind, trying to keep his footing. This was my moment. C'mon, Vesuvius, it's show time.

Suddenly the tremors stopped, and the ground felt eerily silent. Chronos climbed to his feet and stared at me, laughing hysterically at me.

Then, suddenly and without warning—*boom!*

It was the loudest noise I have ever heard or ever hope to hear again, a mighty roar as the mountain exploded skyward in a plume of smoke and ash.

"By Jupiter's thunder! What sorcery is this?" cried one of the vigiles as ash and smoke filled the air. Panic gripped the crowd, their mocking jeers replaced by cries of terror. Even Salvius and his family appeared shaken, holding onto each other amidst the chaos.

"Behold!" I yelled, pointing towards the once-majestic Mount Vesuvius, now spewing forth fire and destruction. "The wrath of Vulcan descends upon us, just as I foretold! This is the end of Pompeii as we know it!"

"Curse you, Iosephus!" Chronos screeched, his eyes wide with fear. "You have brought this calamity upon us!"

"No, Chronos, *you* have!" I shouted back, "I tried to warn you, but you wouldn't listen! The blood of Pompeii is on your hands!"

As the hilltop was swallowed by darkness and the terrible roar of Vesuvius filled our ears, I knew that the time had come to make our escape. For Marcus, Salvius, and his family, and the memories of Pompeii that would live on long after its destruction, we would face the gods' fury and fight for our survival.

The world around us seemed to fracture into chaos. The once-orderly crowd devolved into a stampede of desperate souls, each individual clamoring to escape the wrath of Vesuvius. The air was thick with ash and dust, making it difficult to breathe, let alone see. Every cough, every scream, blended together in a cacophony of terror.

"Run!" I shouted, my voice barely audible above the din of the erupting volcano. "Save yourselves! The end is upon us!" I turned to Marcus. "Marcus!" I shouted, gripping his hand tightly as we stumbled through the whirlwind of panic. "Stay close to me!"

"What is happening, Io?" Marcus cried out, his eyes wide with fear. Despite his confusion, he clung to my hand with unyielding strength—a testament to the love that bound us together.

"Vesuvius has wakened," I explained breathlessly, my heart

pounding in my chest. "We must flee before the gods claim us all!"

I glanced back at the vigiles, who were momentarily distracted by the pandemonium. Seizing the opportunity, I used my knowledge of Roman history to formulate a plan. I remembered reading about how prisoners would sometimes use their bodies as weapons, twisting their limbs to force an escape.

"Listen, Marcus," I said urgently, my voice barely audible above the din. "I need you to help me break free from these restraints."

"But how?" he asked, desperation written across his face.

"Trust me," I replied, driven by the fire in my heart—the love for a man whose life hung in the balance. "We're going to use our bodies as leverage. On my count, twist your arm like this..."

Together, we gritted our teeth and contorted our limbs against the cruel iron shackles. Pain shot through my body, but I refused to give in. I would endure any torment for Marcus for the future we could have together.

"Three... two... one... now!" I commanded, and we wrenched ourselves free with a final surge of strength. The chains that had bound us clattered to the ground, discarded and forgotten.

"By Jupiter's beard!" Marcus exclaimed, his face a mixture of shock and relief. "How did you know that would work?"

"Never mind that now," I said hurriedly. "We have to run!"

With our hands still entwined, we raced down the hillside, dodging panicked citizens and stumbling over debris. My lungs burned, and my legs ached, but the love in my heart propelled me forward.

"Marcus," I whispered between ragged breaths, "no matter what happens, remember this—I love you more than life itself. And I will fight until my last breath to save us both."

"Then we shall face the wrath of the gods together," he replied, determination shining in his eyes. "For I love you just as fiercely, Io."

As we plunged onwards into the swirling darkness, the cries of the damned echoing in our ears, I felt a flicker of hope amidst the chaos. For even in the face of divine retribution, love could still triumph.

We barely made it a few steps down the hill when I spotted Chronos and Ovidius, their eyes wide with terror as they tried to comprehend what was happening. Seizing the opportunity, I stopped and turned to face them, my heart pounding in my chest.

"Look at you!" I shouted, my voice filled with rage and contempt. "You mocked Vulcan and his divine power, and now he sends forth his wrath upon us all! You are to blame for this destruction and the deaths of our fellow citizens!"

"Impossible," Chronos gasped, his skeletal face pale under the dark, ash-filled sky. "We did nothing!"

"Silence!" I snapped, cutting him off. "Your arrogance and disdain for those who dared challenge your so-called wisdom have brought this catastrophe upon us. You thought yourselves untouchable, but even the gods must answer for their actions."

Marcus squeezed my hand as I spoke, his fingers trembling with fear and anger. He glared at the two men, his eyes blazing with righteous fury. "You will pay for the suffering you have caused today," he snarled. "I swear it by Jupiter himself."

The vigiles, who had been momentarily stunned by the sudden eruption and our daring escape, reacted quickly to the drama unfolding before them. As if sensing that Chronos and Ovidius were the true enemies, they closed ranks around the pair, clubbing them and dragging them away from the chaos of the hilltop.

"Traitors!" one of the vigiles spat, kicking Ovidius in the ribs. "You have roused the ire of the gods, and now we all suffer for your wickedness!"

"Have mercy!" Chronos wailed, his high cackling voice now a pitiful whimper. "We did not know!"

"Save your pleas for Pluto," another *vigile* growled, tightening his grip on the old soothsayer's arm. "He'll be the one to decide your fate now."

With Chronos and Ovidius subdued, I turned my attention back to our escape. Marcus and I resumed our frantic flight down the hill, the ash and smoke growing thicker with each passing moment. As we ran, my mind raced with a thousand thoughts—of the history I had studied back in Minneapolis, of the life I had built here in Pompeii, and most importantly, of the man at my side.

"Marcus," I whispered as we stumbled through the darkness, "no matter what happens, remember this—I love you more than life itself. And I will fight until my last breath to save us both."

"Then we shall face the wrath of the gods together," he replied, determination shining in his eyes. "For I love you just as fiercely, Io."

As Marcus and I raced down the hillside, my heart hammered in my chest, a relentless drumbeat urging us to flee. Ash fell like gray snow, coating everything in a thick layer of despair. And yet, amid the chaos and destruction, there was a glimmer of hope— for Salvius and his family had joined us in our desperate escape.

"Keep moving!" Salvius shouted through the cacophony of screams and crumbling buildings. His wife clutched their youngest child tightly, her eyes wide with terror, while their older children struggled to keep up on unsteady legs.

"Stay together!" I called back, the ash making it difficult to breathe. I glanced at Marcus, his dark curls now streaked with gray, his face set in grim determination. He nodded at me as if to say, We'll make it through this.

As we continued our frantic flight from the erupting volcano, I couldn't help but think of all the historical facts I had taught my students about Pompeii—the bustling marketplace, the vibrant frescoes, and the intricate mosaics. It pained me to know that such beauty would soon be lost forever beneath a blanket of ash and pumice.

"Look out!" Marcus suddenly cried, pulling me back just in time to avoid being crushed by a collapsing building. The once-sturdy structure crumbled before us like a sandcastle washed away by an unforgiving tide, its bricks and mortar reduced to little more than dust.

"By the gods," Salvius gasped, staring at the destruction with wide, disbelieving eyes. "What have we done to deserve such wrath?"

"Perhaps Vulcan has finally grown tired of our hubris," I suggested, remembering a quote from Seneca. "We thought ourselves invincible, masters of an eternal empire, when in truth, we were but insects scurrying beneath the feet of giants."

"Then let us scurry while we still can," Marcus said grimly, grabbing my hand and pulling me onward. "We have no time for philosophical musings—only survival."

As we continued our harrowing descent down the hill, I could hear the cries of those less fortunate than ourselves—people trapped beneath rubble, their screams muffled by the relentless ash, or lost in the smoke-choked darkness, calling out in vain for loved ones they would never see again.

"Stay close!" Salvius yelled back to his family, fear etching deep lines in his normally jovial face. "We must make it to the harbor—it may be our only chance!"

"Right behind you!" I shouted, struggling to keep up as we navigated the treacherous terrain. My lungs burned with each labored breath, and my legs ached from the strain, but there was no time for rest, no respite from the nightmare that had engulfed our once-thriving city.

"Marcus," I panted as we ran, "no matter what happens, remember this—" But he silenced me with a fierce, determined look.

"Save your breath, Io," he said, squeezing my hand tighter. "We'll have time for declarations of love when we're safe. Now run!"

And so we ran, side by side, our fates intertwined like the ivy that had once climbed the walls of Pompeii—a city now doomed to be buried by history, its beauty, and grandeur consigned to the annals of time, a fading memory amidst the relentless march of empires.

The deafening roar of Vesuvius, coupled with the frantic cries of the fleeing citizens, created a cacophony that seemed to tear at the very fabric of the world. We raced down the hillside, ash, and pumice raining down upon us, obscuring our vision and choking our breaths. Yet amidst the chaos and devastation, there was an inexplicable bond between us—Salvius, his family, Marcus, and me—as we ran for our lives.

"By Jupiter!" Salvius suddenly shouted, skidding to a halt and turning back to gaze upon the city he had called home for so many years. I could see the heartbreak etched upon his face as he watched in horror while Pompeii crumbled beneath the wrath of the angry mountain.

"Salvius," I gasped, my chest heaving as I tried to catch my breath. "We have to keep moving!"

"Look at it, Io," he whispered, tears streaming down his cheeks as he stared at the once-majestic city being swallowed by the infernal storm. "How can this be happening?"

I placed a hand on his shoulder, struggling to find words that might offer some comfort. "Pompeii will not be forgotten," I murmured, my voice barely audible over the din of destruction. "Someday, people will unearth its ruins, learn about its history, and marvel at its wonders."

Salvius turned to regard me, his eyes filled with a mixture of pain and curiosity. "Who are you?" he asked, his voice hoarse from inhaling the acrid fumes that choked the air.

"Salvius now is not the time," Marcus interjected, his own face streaked with sweat, ash, and unshed tears. "We must get to the harbor—it's our only hope!"

"Marcus is right," I agreed, my heart aching for the man who had shown us such kindness and generosity in a city now lost to time. "We can mourn for Pompeii later, but for now, we need to survive."

"Very well," Salvius conceded, his eyes lingering on the dying city for just a moment longer before he nodded, determination replacing despair. "Let us go, then—and may the gods have mercy on us all."

As we resumed our desperate flight, I couldn't help but feel a sense of responsibility for this tragedy—for I had traveled through time and found love in an era not meant for me, and now it seemed as though the very fabric of history was unraveling around us. But like the fabled phoenix rising from the ashes, we too would find a way to rebuild, to forge a new life amidst the ruins of the past.

And so, hand in hand, Marcus and I ran toward an uncertain future, propelled by love, hope, and the indomitable spirit that defined the citizens of Pompeii—a city whose memory would endure through the ages, a testament to the resilience of the human heart.

As we raced down the hillside, ash, and smoke billowing around us, I saw a mixture of terror and curiosity in the eyes of those we passed. People who had once been our neighbors, friends, and even enemies—all now united in the face of impending doom. In that moment, I realized that while Pompeii might be lost to history, its people would live on through the bonds of love and friendship forged in this time of crisis.

Suddenly a hand reached out and grabbed me from behind. I fell backward, coming face to face with Chronos, who now stood over me. Behind him, I could see the cloud of hot ash and fire coming toward us. "There is no escape for either of us, Iosephus! You will perish with the rest of us."

"Kiss my ass!" I said in English as I pulled myself up and lunged at Chronos. We struggled on top of that hill as the cloud of death sped closer and closer. I glanced over just long enough to see that Marcus and the others were getting away, then I turned to Chronos. Suddenly everything was clear.

"You brought me here!" I shouted at him in English. "If you really have the power you say you'd understand my words!"

"Your Celtic curses will not work on me."

"Here's a Celtic curse for you, Chronos: *fuck you!*" With that I reached forward and grabbed the amulet, yanking it off of him. I held on tightly, even though it felt like I had grabbed on to a high-voltage power line, and fell back as the pyroclastic flow overtook us both....

EPILOGVE

I woke up with the bright sun shining down on my face, covered in sweat. I opened my eyes to see Kerrie slowly coming into focus. She was looking down at me, her eyes full of concern. "Joe?" she asked me, "are you okay?"

I sat up and looked around, trying to get my bearings. I was back in my own time! Pompeii was a devastated ruin now that surrounded me. I threw my arms around my old friend. "Oh my gods! Kerrie! Is it really you?"

"What are you talking about? You passed out," Kerrie explained, handing me a bottle of cold water. "We were all worried about you. Here, drink this."

"I just had the strangest dream," I said, pulling myself up to sit on a stone. "But it couldn't have been a dream. It was too real to be a dream."

"What are you talking about?"

"I was there, Kerrie. I was in Pompeii."

"Of course, you were. You still are."

"No, I mean *old* Pompeii—before the eruption! I was there! I met the people there! They called me Iosephus Andrius. I met Tacitus, and Pliny! I saw what the mountain looked like before it erupted." I smiled at a memory. "I made love on top of the mountain… under the stars."

"Sounds like a vivid dream."

"I don't think it was a dream, Kerrie. It was all so real… and I was there for almost a year. I tried to warn people, but most of them wouldn't listen."

"You tried to change history?"

"I was more concerned about not becoming part of history, if ya know what I mean." I could tell by the look on her face that she didn't believe me. "It's gotta be this thing." I held up the amulet. "I found it lying on the ground where the diggers were working."

"A seven-pointed star?" Kerrie asked. "The mathematics involved in designing something like this are staggering…"

"The stone at the center was green," I pointed out, "and it glowed, like it had a light bulb inside." Now the stone was dark and cracked. It had no power now. "When I picked it up, it was like grabbing a live wire. Suddenly I was in old Pompeii and ev'rybody was speaking Latin."

Kerrie shook her head. Apparently, she wasn't buying my story. Would you? As I re-accustomed myself to living in the present, I was starting to wonder about it myself.

Then I remembered Marcus. He was gone now, of course, but at least I had the satisfaction of knowing that he had escaped the destruction of Pompeii, along with Salvius and his household. He was long dead, but his life had probably been a little longer because I saved him in Pompeii, if he ever existed at all. I looked over at the fresco of him on the wall, remembering the feel of his touch and the taste of his lips, and brushed a tear from my eye. We were doomed from the start, I figured. He was a ghost from the past, while I was a spectre from the future. It was never meant to be.

"There you are!" Niles found us and beckoned us to follow him. "Cal finally got that chamber open. You're gonna have to see this to believe it."

I smirked as Kerrie helped me to my feet, knowing what Niles was talking about. I let her walk in first. The room had been sealed in darkness for 1,939 years, but now it was lit up by Smith's L.E.D. lantern.

Cal was staring at the mural on the wall with a sneer. "Well, I'll be a son of a bitch."

Kerrie walked into the room and gasped. "Oh my god!"

The chamber was a simple room with a simple bed, sealed in darkness for almost two millennia and now illuminated by L.E.D. lanterns.

What made the room remarkable were two paintings hanging on the wall, full-figure nudes that left nothing to the imagination. One was a painting of Marcus, in all his naked glory. The other was even more familiar, almost embarrassingly so.

It was Niles who noticed first, pointing to the painting on the right. "That's different," he noted. "Of all the erotic art we've seen, this is the only one that shows a circumcised penis. Perhaps a Judean slave?"

Kerrie wasn't looking at the penis. She was more interested in the face in the painting. Quintus had done a good job of capturing my likeness. "My god," Kerrie gasped, "it's you, Joe!" Quintus had even included our names on each canvas: Marcus Andronicus and Iosephus Andrius.

"Iosephus Andrius," Kerrie realized. She grabbed me by the arm and dragged me out of the chamber to where we could speak in private. "Spill it, Joe," she demanded. "What the fuck is going on here?"

"I told you," I said. "I don't understand it any more than you do. But it must have been this." I pulled the amulet out of my pocket. The stone was crumbling away. "I picked it up over there, and I found myself in Pompeii. When I snatched it off of Chronos, I came back." I looked at it, shaking my head. "I think it's lost any power it had."

"You can't keep it." She told me. "You know that, right? It's an antiquity." She looked down the street as if to make sure nobody was looking. "The local law enforcement has been cracking down on us today... it seems several of the plaster casts they made of the bodies have gone missing. I can't imagine why anyone would want to steal them."

"Maybe they weren't stolen," I posed. "Not everybody in Pompeii thought I was insane. A few believed me and escaped before the end. Those plaster casts weren't stolen; those were people I saved from the volcano."

"It just doesn't make any sense, Joe. The painting... that amulet... but it's not possible! We're scientists, Joe!"

"Science doesn't have all the answers," I shrugged. "I have no idea what happened, but now that I'm back, I don't miss it." That was a lie. "Except one thing I miss."

"The man in the other painting, I presume."

"Yeah, Marcus. He was the one who helped me get used to living in

Pompeii. I might have been passed out for a few minutes to you, but I was there for over a year. I'm surprised I can still speak English I've been speaking Latin for so long." Thinking about Marcus made me sad. He was lost to the ages now, nothing more than a memory that never should have been.

"So were you right?" Kerrie asked with a smirk, snapping me out of my reverie. "Did your school-learned Latin make them think you were a snob?"

"They thought I was some wise man. It wasn't hard to keep up the ruse, I had almost two millennia of philosophy to call upon. And George Carlin sounds so much cooler in Latin. *Non minoris aestimo potestatem multorum stulti.*"

* * *

There's no feeling quite like finally getting home after a long vacation, and that had been the longest vacation of my life. I had to re-acquaint myself with Minneapolis as we made our way from the airport to my brownstone. It was just as I had left it two weeks earlier, though over a year had passed for me. Dr. Baker, the crazy old physics professor I knew back in college was right when he said that if you thought about time travel too much, it'd give you a headache. And I had the mother of all headaches.

As I made my way up the stairs to my apartment, I tapped on Mike's door, but there was no answer. I figured I could catch up with him later. I was just too tired to deal with his antics right now. All I wanted to do was to take a hot shower, eat some takeout and sleep in my own bed.

But as soon as I opened the door to my apartment, I knew something was off. There was a musky scent in the air that I didn't recognize, and Felix was nowhere in sight. I called out his name, and a gentle meow responded. I turned to see a stranger standing there, cradling the kitty in his arms. Felix usually hates being held.

That's when I heard a familiar voice. "Hi," the deep voice said, "You must be Joe. I'm your new neighbor. I'm—"

"Marcus?" It was Marcus, right down to his endearing smile and chocolate brown eyes! But this wasn't possible!

The stranger grinned. Even his smile was the same. "Wow," he smiled. "Nobody's called me that in ages." He reached out and touched my upper arm and I felt a spark pass between us. His eyes moved down then out, clearly checking me out, and he smiled approvingly. "Anyway, Mike had a death in the family, so he asked me to look after your cat. He didn't think you'd mind." His brow furrowed. "You look... familiar. Do I know you?"

"I don't think so," I lied, looking into his deep, familiar brown eyes and smiling. "Though I'm pretty sure I've seen you before." About two millennia ago, but I kept that to myself. "Anyway, welcome to the building. We should, I dunno... hang out sometime?"

Marcus thought about it for a moment. "You just got home from vacation, you prob'ly don't feel like cooking. Wanna order a pizza," he smiled, and... I dunno... hang out?"

"Yeah," I smiled. "That'd be cool. I'll buy."

"Awesome. I've got some beer in the fridge, I'll go get it... and by the way, I go by Marc... with a c."

I settled into my favorite chair and smiled, looking up at him with a wink. "Marcus it is, then."

TERMINVS

ABOVT THE AVTHOR

Matt Butts was born in New Orleans, and
attended Benjamin Franklin High School for two
years before transferring to Marion Abramson
Senior High School, where he wrote for his
school newspaper and acted in school plays. After
high school, Matt took up space at the University

of New Orleans for two semesters, where he hung around the
campus paper and majored in substance abuse. Matt left New
Orleans at age 20 and moved to Minneapolis, where he came out
of the closet at the tender young age of 26. Matt found his niche as
a homojournalist, learning typesetting on the side and eventually
starting his own newspaper in 1991. Matt retired from his "day
job" in the mortgage industry just in the nick of time, right before
the big crash in 2008. His first novel, *Grunch Road*, was published
in 2011. Matt lives in a suburb of Minneapolis with his roommate
Jim, whom everybody thinks is his husband (he isn't*) and sings
baritone with the Twin Cities Gay Men's Chorus.

---

* *Oh god, no! He talks in his sleep!*

Bromance Novels
by Matt Butts

Love at Second Sight

Adam Weiser may seem like just another pretty face at the gay bar, but behind his sparkling blue eyes lurks a power he doesn't understand and can't control: he's a telepath, able to hear people's thoughts and learn everything about them with a look in their eye. It's a secret he keeps even from his closest friends. But when a trio of hateful teens attacks him and kills his newfound friend, Adam's not afraid to use his power to get justice... and win the heart of the officer assigned to his case, who's *falling in love with him!*

Teach Me to Fly

Colin Manning is the dorkiest, nerdiest kid in the senior class at Emerson High School. But don't underestimate him: he was born in the eye of a hurricane and survived every storm life threw at him, armed only with his mother's love. They've pulled up stakes and moved to Minnesota to escape Florida's book bans and "don't say gay" laws. Colin is making new friends at his new school... and an enemy or two. Like Brad Wolf, the arrogant captain of the basketball team who's locked in an internal struggle nobody knows about. But Brad's suppressed emotions come boiling to the surface when a school shooter has him at point-blank range... and *Colin is the unlikely hero who saves his life!*

What Happens in Pompeii

Joe Andrews is a history teacher passionate about anything related to the Roman Empire. So when an old friend invites him to explore the ancient city of Pompeii, he jumps at the chance. Touring the ruins is a Romanophile's dream... until a shiny object catches Joe's eye, and when he picks up a strange amulet, he's suddenly thrown back in time to the year 78, a year before the city's destruction. With no way home, he adapts to life in Pompeii, finding love with a wealthy businessman's servant. Joe could live happily ever after with Marcus, except the town's official seer despises him, a secretive cult wants to recruit him, and there's a ticking time bomb towering over the city, a sleeping giant about to awaken....

Wish You Were Here

Artist Luke Brody thought he had found happily ever after with Brian, his first love. But cancer took Brian away, leaving Luke a lonely and broken man haunted by visions of his lost lover's ghost. Then he meets J.D., a free-spirited young man intent on tearing down the wall Luke has built around himself and helping him find happiness again. But before he can find new happiness with J.D., Luke must bury his dead once and for all.

Support a Starving Artist and buy them all!

All titles available in Hardcover, Paperback and Kindle™ editions.

available at
amazon